THE BRAVE AND THE BOLD.

STONE ARCH BOOKS
a capstone imprint

STONE ARCH BOOKS™
Published in 2012
A Capstone Imprint
1710 Roe Crest Drive
North Mankato, MN 56003
www.capstonepub.com

Originally published by DC Comics in
the U.S. in single magazine form as
Batman: The Brave and the Bold #4.

DC Comics
1700 Broadway, New York, NY 10019
A Warner Bros. Entertainment Company

Cataloging-in-Publication Data is available at the
Library of Congress website:
ISBN: 978-1-4342-4548-9 (library binding)

Summary: Batman studies the past, but he never expected to be part of history! Now, thanks to the Time Lord known as Rip Hunter, Batman and Aquaman might never return to the present!

STONE ARCH BOOKS
Ashley C. Andersen Zantop *Publisher*
Michael Dahl *Editorial Director*
Donald Lemke & Christianne Jones *Editors*
Heather Kindseth *Creative Director*
Hilary Wacholz *Designer*
Kathy McColley *Production Specialist*

DC COMICS
Rachel Gluckstern & Michael Siglain *Original U.S. Editors*
Harvey Richards *U.S. Assistant Editor*
James Tucker *Cover Artist*

Printed in the United States of America
in Brainerd, Minnesota.
032012 006672BANGF12

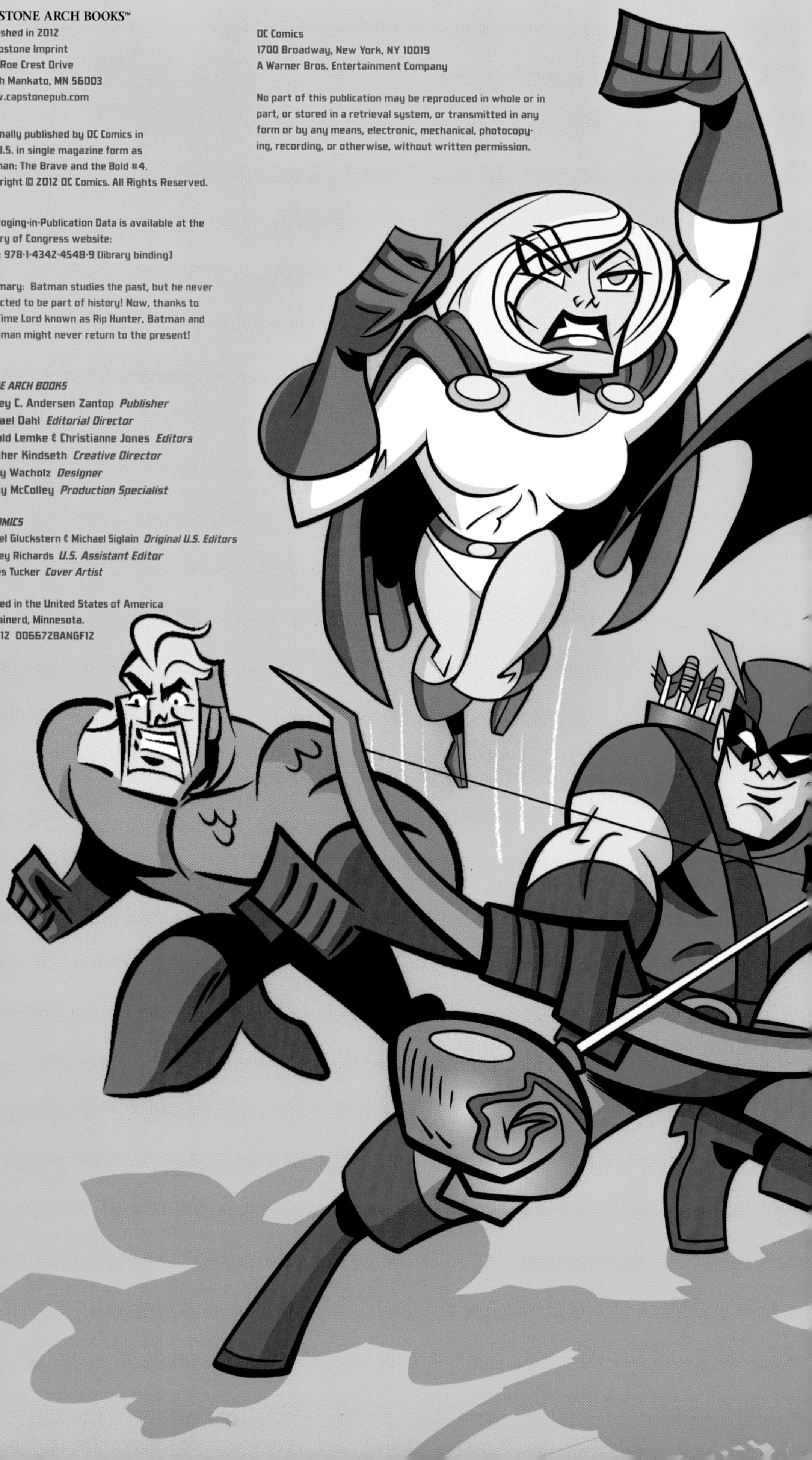

BATMAN
THE BRAVE AND THE BOLD®

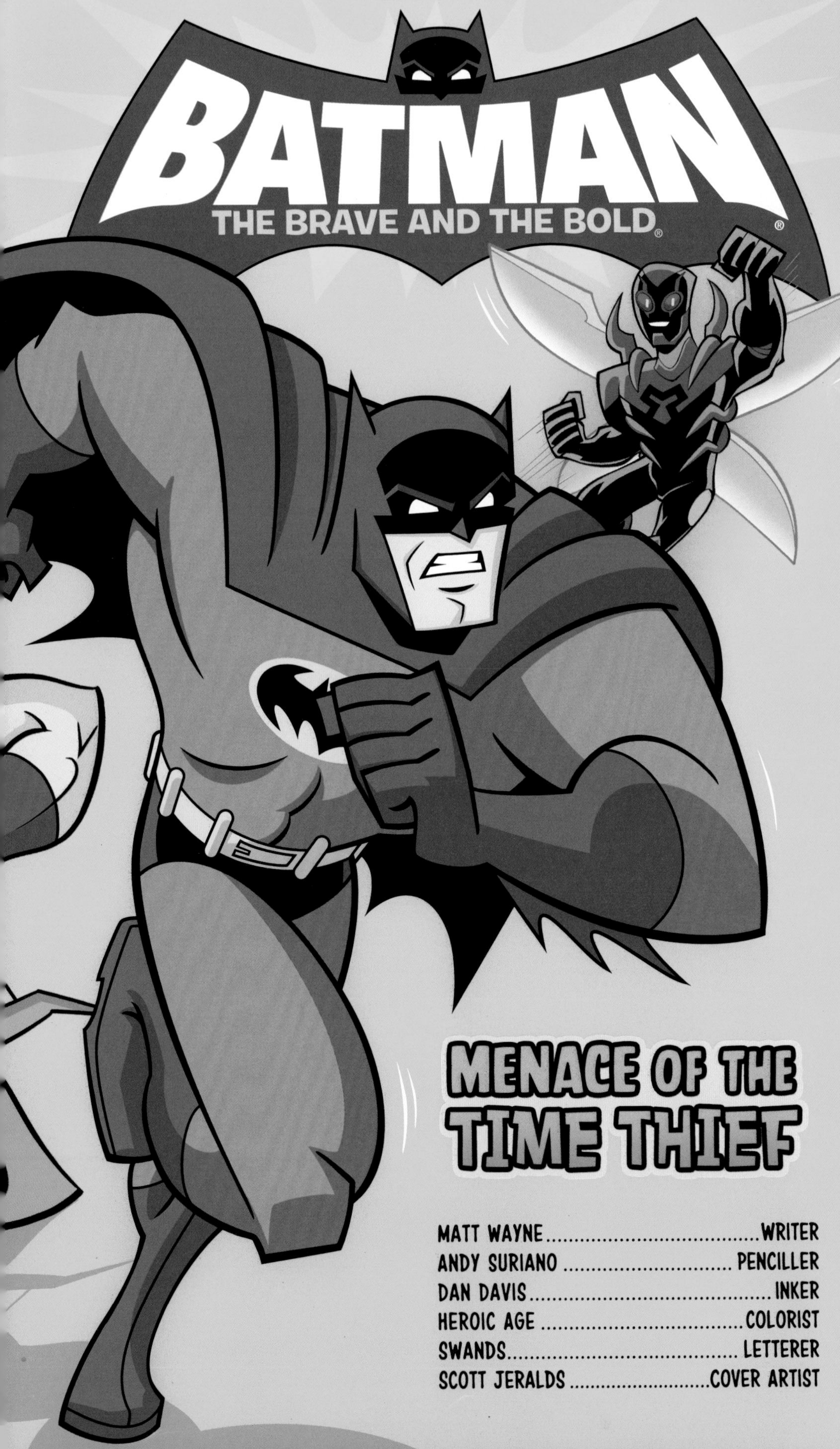

MENACE OF THE TIME THIEF

MATT WAYNE.......................................WRITER
ANDY SURIANO ....PENCILLER
DAN DAVIS...INKER
HEROIC AGE ....COLORIST
SWANDS...LETTERER
SCOTT JERALDS ....COVER ARTIST

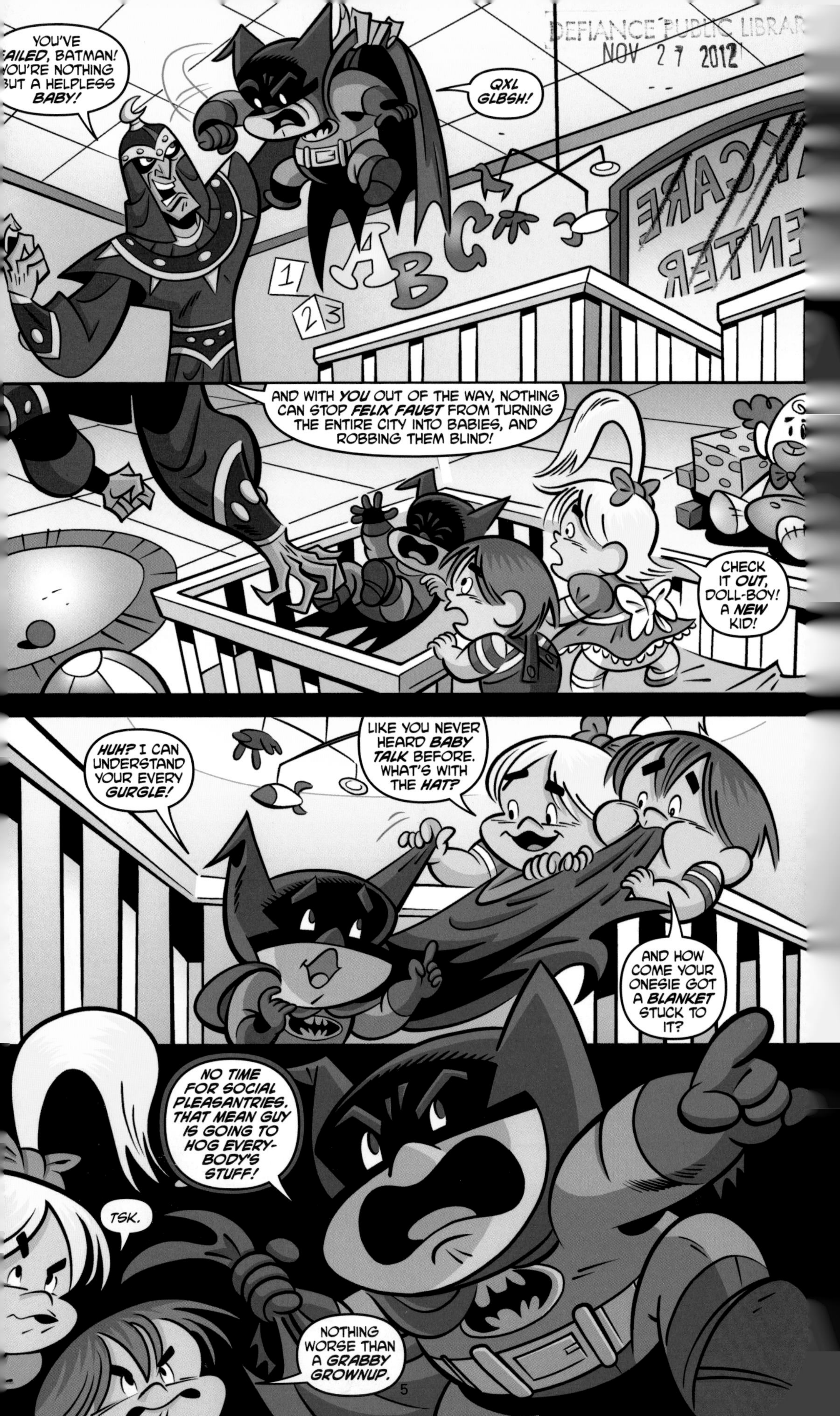

YOU'VE FAILED, BATMAN! YOU'RE NOTHING BUT A HELPLESS BABY!
QXL GLBSH!
AND WITH YOU OUT OF THE WAY, NOTHING CAN STOP FELIX FAUST FROM TURNING THE ENTIRE CITY INTO BABIES, AND ROBBING THEM BLIND!
CHECK IT OUT, DOLL-BOY! A NEW KID!
HUH? I CAN UNDERSTAND YOUR EVERY GURGLE!
LIKE YOU NEVER HEARD BABY TALK BEFORE. WHAT'S WITH THE HAT?
AND HOW COME YOUR ONESIE GOT A BLANKET STUCK TO IT?
NO TIME FOR SOCIAL PLEASANTRIES. THAT MEAN GUY IS GOING TO HOG EVERY-BODY'S STUFF!
TSK.
NOTHING WORSE THAN A GRABBY GROWNUP.

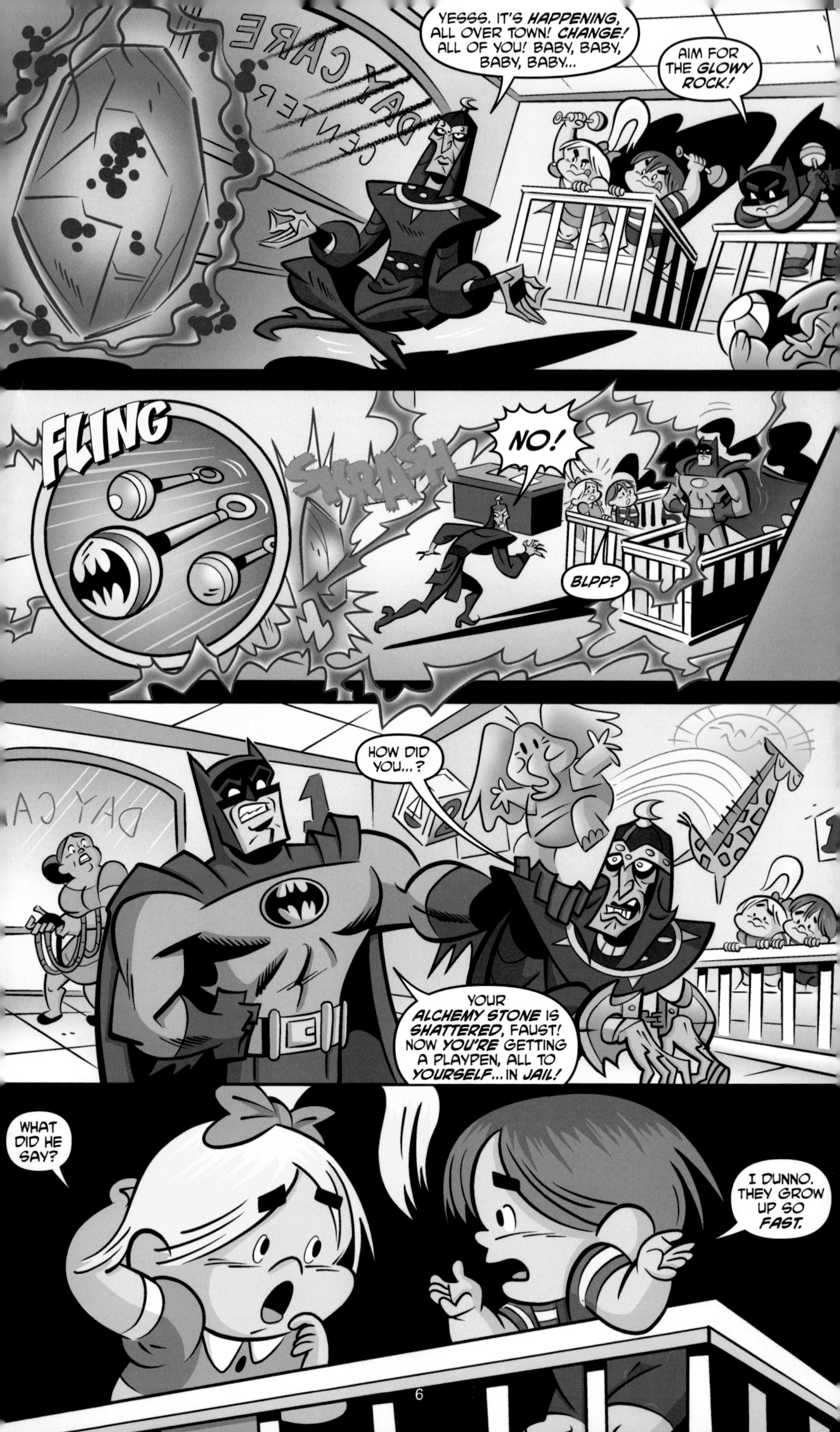
DAY CARE CENTER
YESSS. IT'S HAPPENING, ALL OVER TOWN! CHANGE! ALL OF YOU! BABY, BABY, BABY, BABY...
AIM FOR THE GLOWY ROCK!
FLING
SKRASH
NO!
BLPP?
HOW DID YOU...?
YOUR ALCHEMY STONE IS SHATTERED, FAUST! NOW YOU'RE GETTING A PLAYPEN, ALL TO YOURSELF...IN JAIL!
WHAT DID HE SAY?
I DUNNO. THEY GROW UP SO FAST.

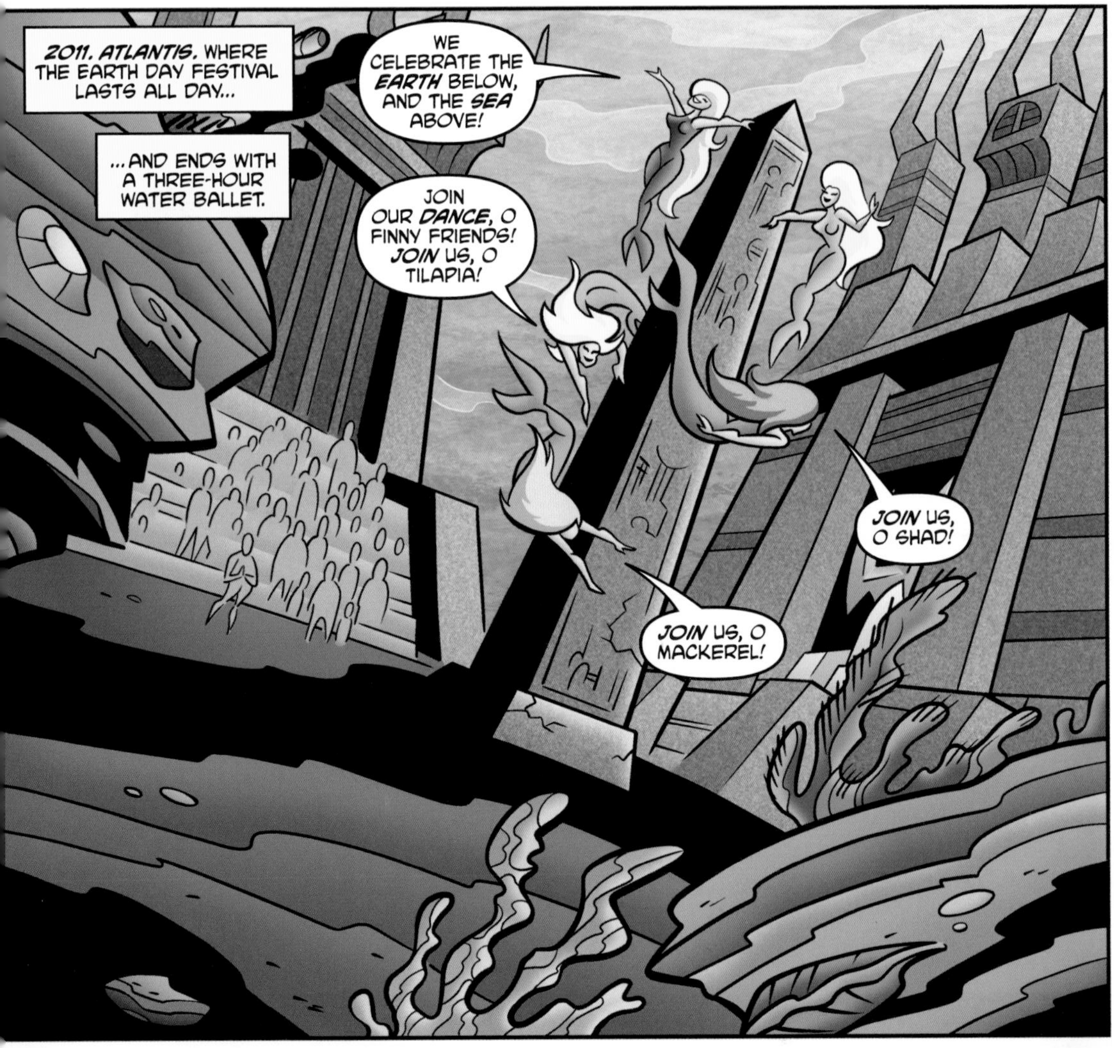
2011. ATLANTIS. WHERE THE EARTH DAY FESTIVAL LASTS ALL DAY...
...AND ENDS WITH A THREE-HOUR WATER BALLET.
WE CELEBRATE THE EARTH BELOW, AND THE SEA ABOVE!
JOIN OUR DANCE, O FINNY FRIENDS! JOIN US, O TILAPIA!
JOIN US, O SHAD!
JOIN US, O MACKEREL!

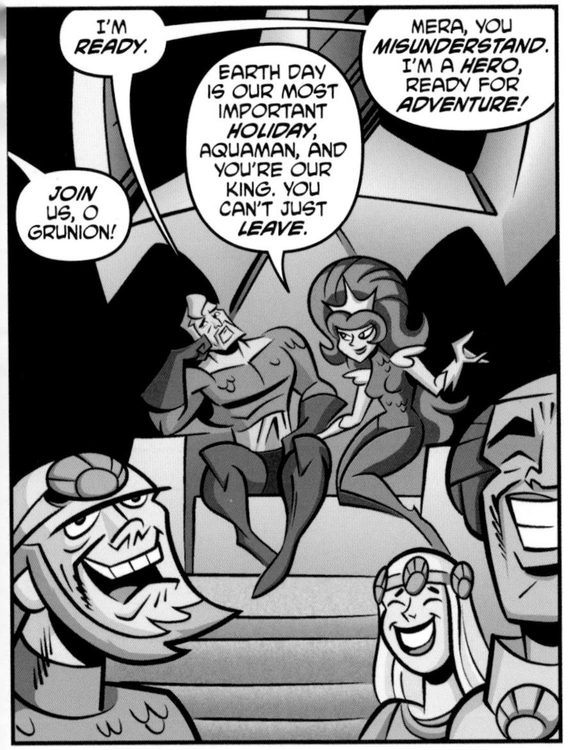
JOIN US, O GRUNION!
I'M READY.
EARTH DAY IS OUR MOST IMPORTANT HOLIDAY, AQUAMAN, AND YOU'RE OUR KING. YOU CAN'T JUST LEAVE.
MERA, YOU MISUNDERSTAND. I'M A HERO, READY FOR ADVENTURE!

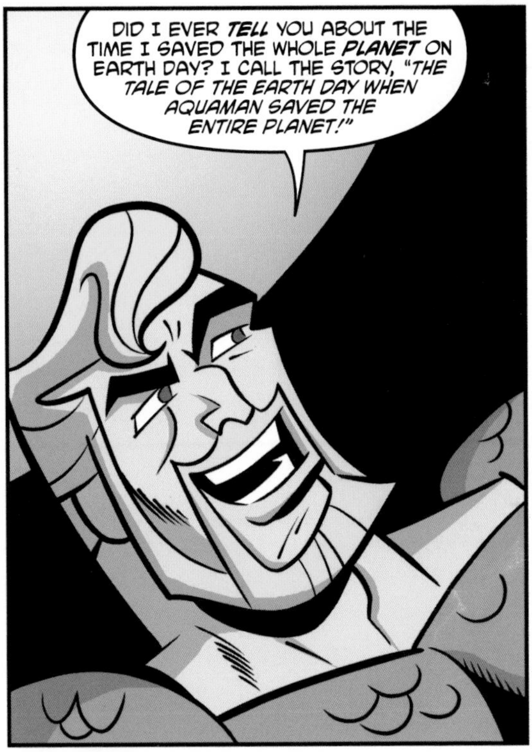
DID I EVER TELL YOU ABOUT THE TIME I SAVED THE WHOLE PLANET ON EARTH DAY? I CALL THE STORY, "THE TALE OF THE EARTH DAY WHEN AQUAMAN SAVED THE ENTIRE PLANET!"

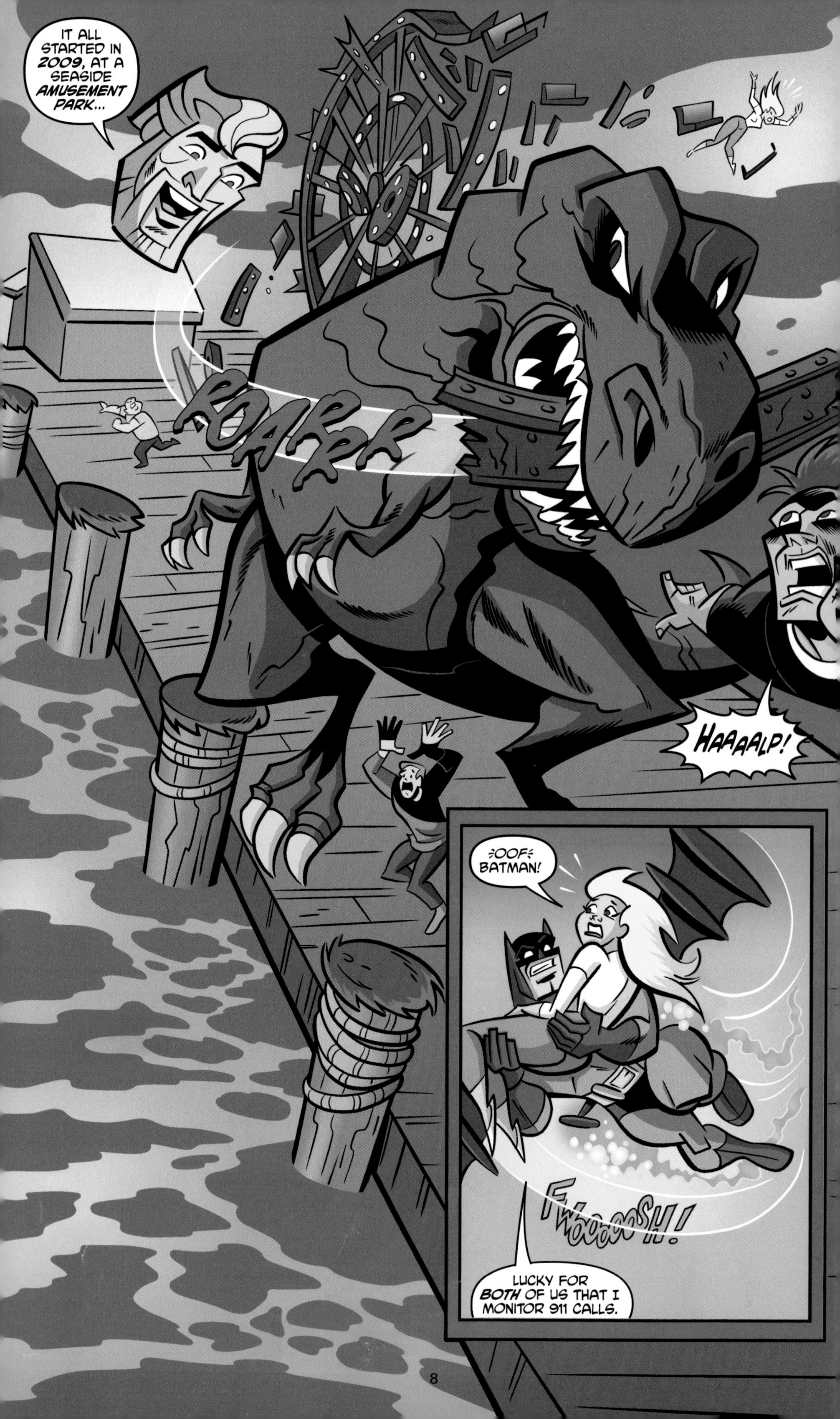

IT ALL STARTED IN 2009, AT A SEASIDE AMUSEMENT PARK...
ROARRR
HAAAALP!
OOF BATMAN!
FWOOOOSH!
LUCKY FOR BOTH OF US THAT I MONITOR 911 CALLS.

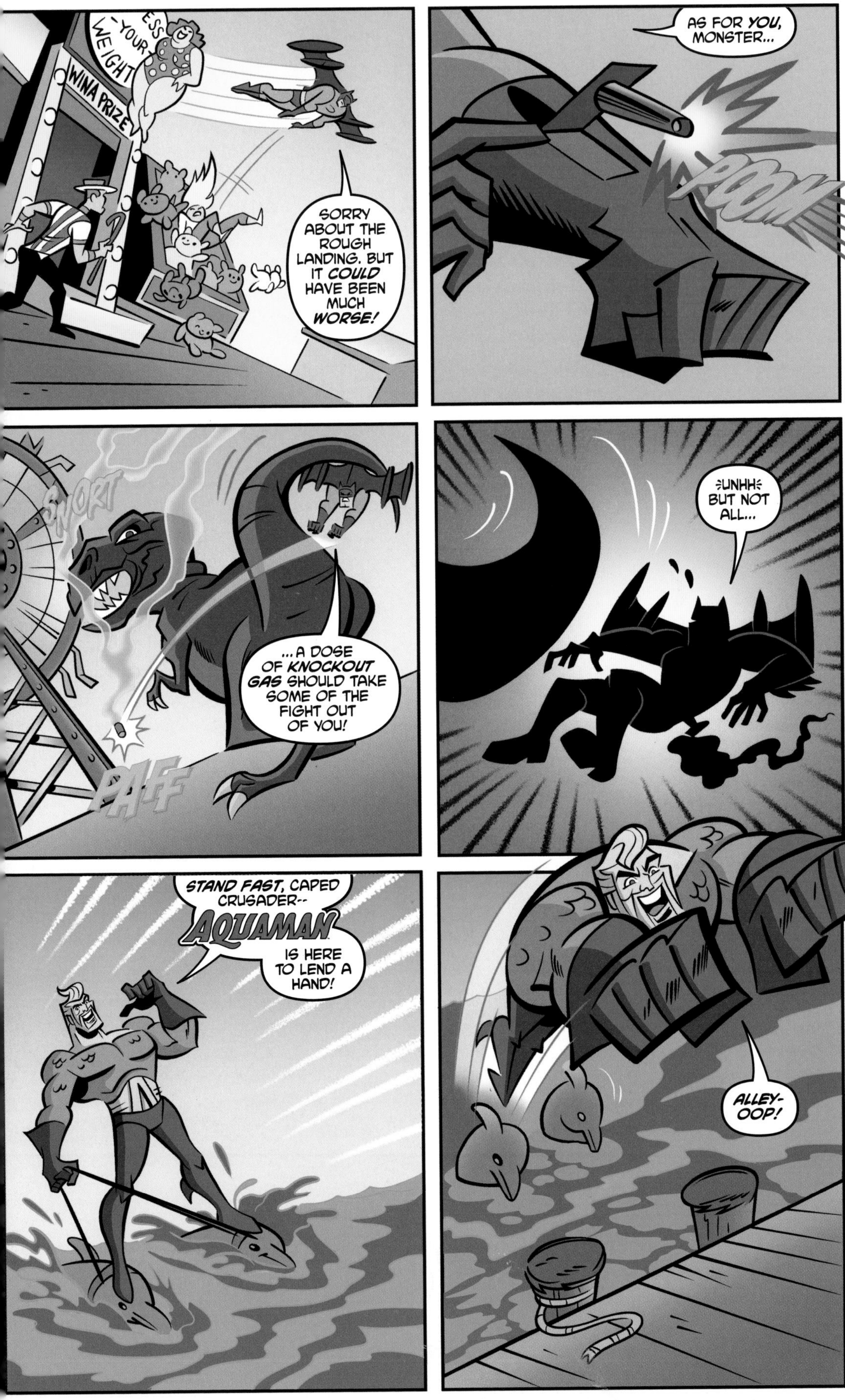
GUESS YOUR WEIGHT
WIN A PRIZE
SORRY ABOUT THE ROUGH LANDING. BUT IT COULD HAVE BEEN MUCH WORSE!
AS FOR YOU, MONSTER...
POOM
SNORT
...A DOSE OF KNOCKOUT GAS SHOULD TAKE SOME OF THE FIGHT OUT OF YOU!
PAFF
UNHH BUT NOT ALL...
STAND FAST, CAPED CRUSADER-- AQUAMAN IS HERE TO LEND A HAND!
ALLEY-OOP!

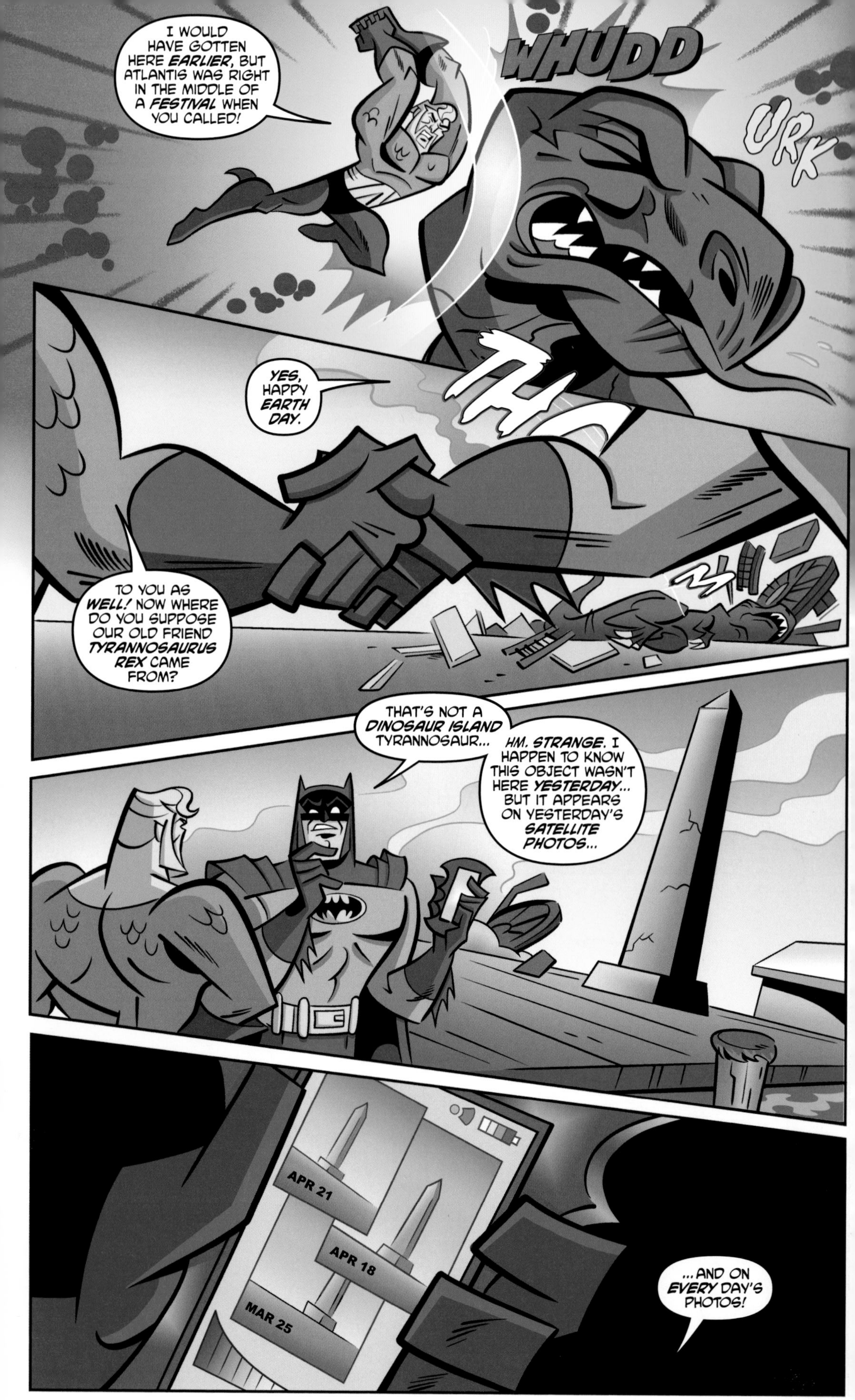
I WOULD HAVE GOTTEN HERE EARLIER, BUT ATLANTIS WAS RIGHT IN THE MIDDLE OF A FESTIVAL WHEN YOU CALLED!
WHUDD
ORK
YES, HAPPY EARTH DAY.
TH
TO YOU AS WELL! NOW WHERE DO YOU SUPPOSE OUR OLD FRIEND TYRANNOSAURUS REX CAME FROM?
THAT'S NOT A DINOSAUR ISLAND TYRANNOSAUR...
HM. STRANGE. I HAPPEN TO KNOW THIS OBJECT WASN'T HERE YESTERDAY... BUT IT APPEARS ON YESTERDAY'S SATELLITE PHOTOS...
APR 21
APR 18
MAR 25
...AND ON EVERY DAY'S PHOTOS!

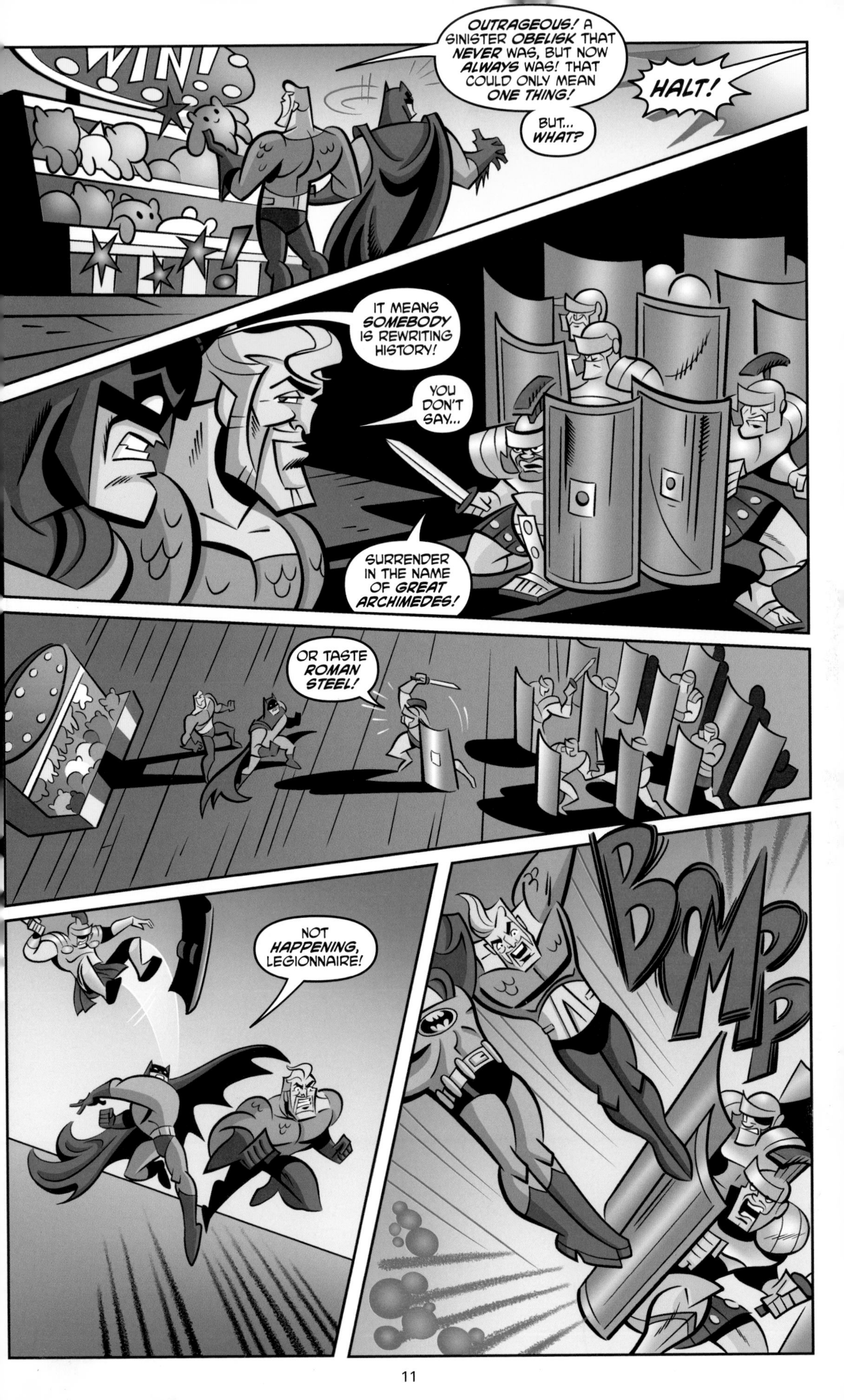

OUTRAGEOUS! A SINISTER OBELISK THAT NEVER WAS, BUT NOW ALWAYS WAS! THAT COULD ONLY MEAN ONE THING!
BUT... WHAT?
HALT!
IT MEANS SOMEBODY IS REWRITING HISTORY!
YOU DON'T SAY...
SURRENDER IN THE NAME OF GREAT ARCHIMEDES!
OR TASTE ROMAN STEEL!
NOT HAPPENING, LEGIONNAIRE!
BOMP

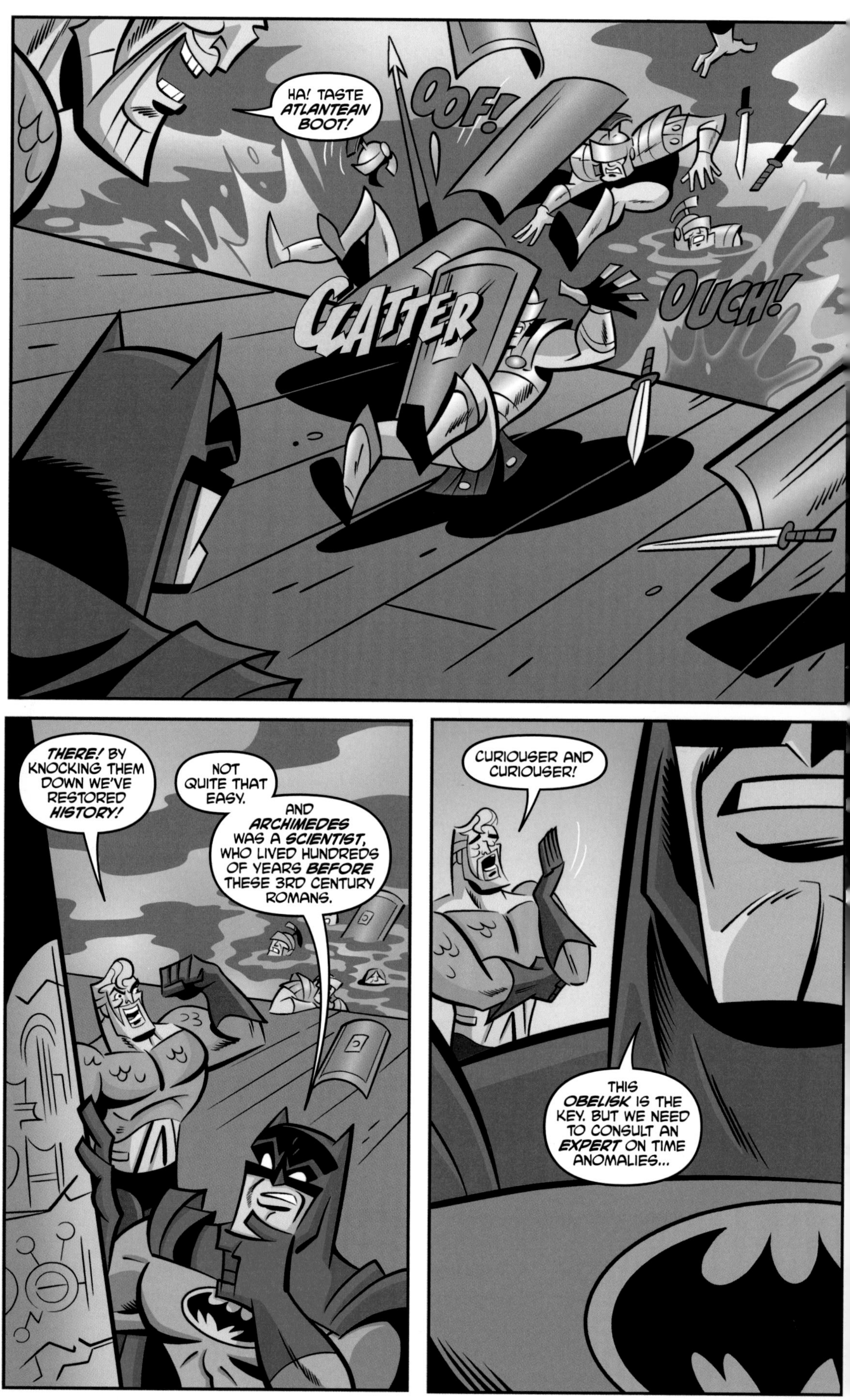

HA! TASTE ATLANTEAN BOOT!
OOF!
CLATTER
OUCH!
THERE! BY KNOCKING THEM DOWN WE'VE RESTORED HISTORY!
NOT QUITE THAT EASY.
AND ARCHIMEDES WAS A SCIENTIST, WHO LIVED HUNDREDS OF YEARS BEFORE THESE 3RD CENTURY ROMANS.
CURIOUSER AND CURIOUSER!
THIS OBELISK IS THE KEY. BUT WE NEED TO CONSULT AN EXPERT ON TIME ANOMALIES...

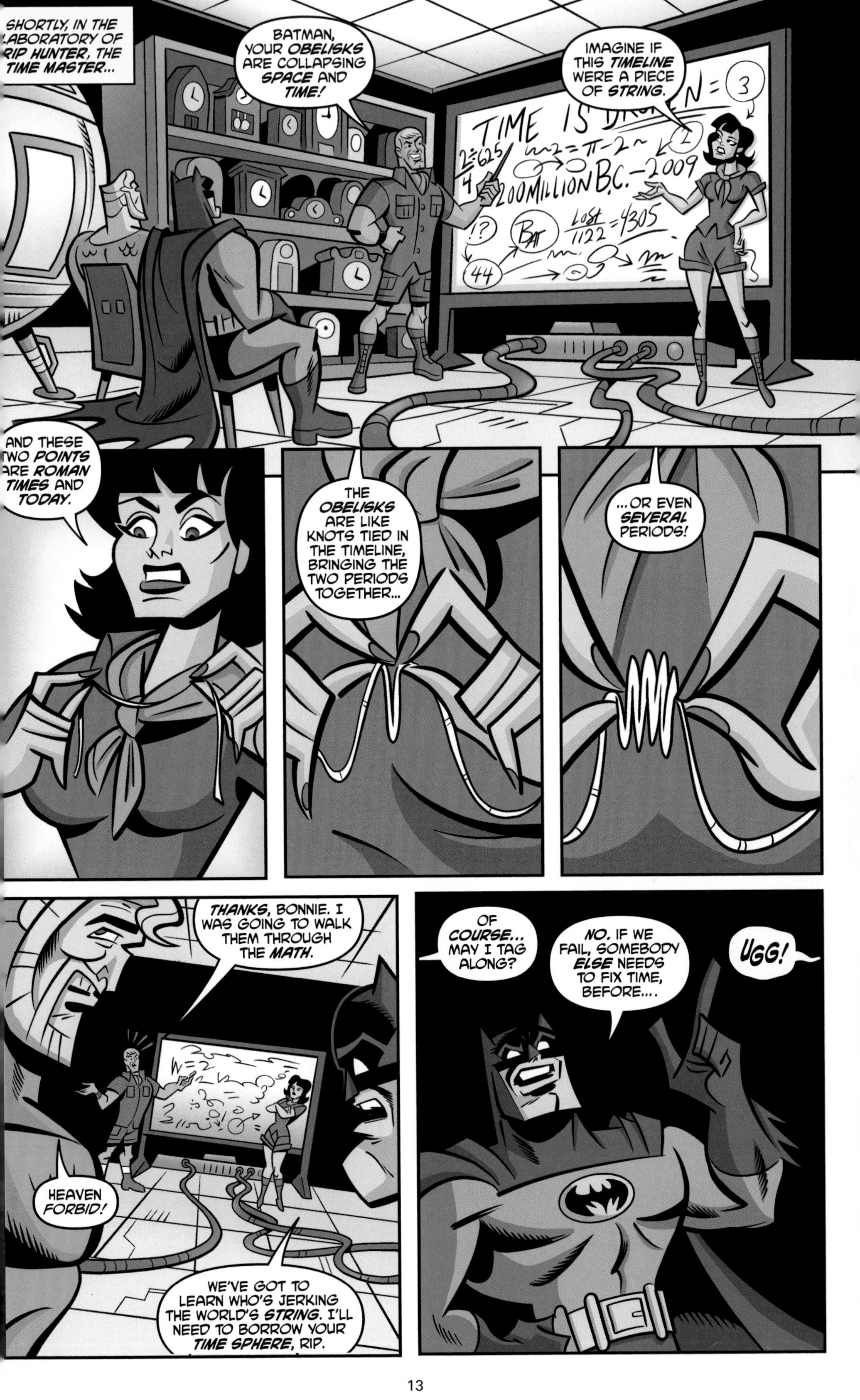

SHORTLY, IN THE LABORATORY OF RIP HUNTER, THE TIME MASTER...
BATMAN, YOUR OBELISKS ARE COLLAPSING SPACE AND TIME!
IMAGINE IF THIS TIMELINE WERE A PIECE OF STRING.
AND THESE TWO POINTS ARE ROMAN TIMES AND TODAY.
THE OBELISKS ARE LIKE KNOTS TIED IN THE TIMELINE, BRINGING THE TWO PERIODS TOGETHER...
...OR EVEN SEVERAL PERIODS!
THANKS, BONNIE. I WAS GOING TO WALK THEM THROUGH THE MATH.
HEAVEN FORBID!
WE'VE GOT TO LEARN WHO'S JERKING THE WORLD'S STRING. I'LL NEED TO BORROW YOUR TIME SPHERE, RIP.
OF COURSE... MAY I TAG ALONG?
NO. IF WE FAIL, SOMEBODY ELSE NEEDS TO FIX TIME, BEFORE....
UGG!

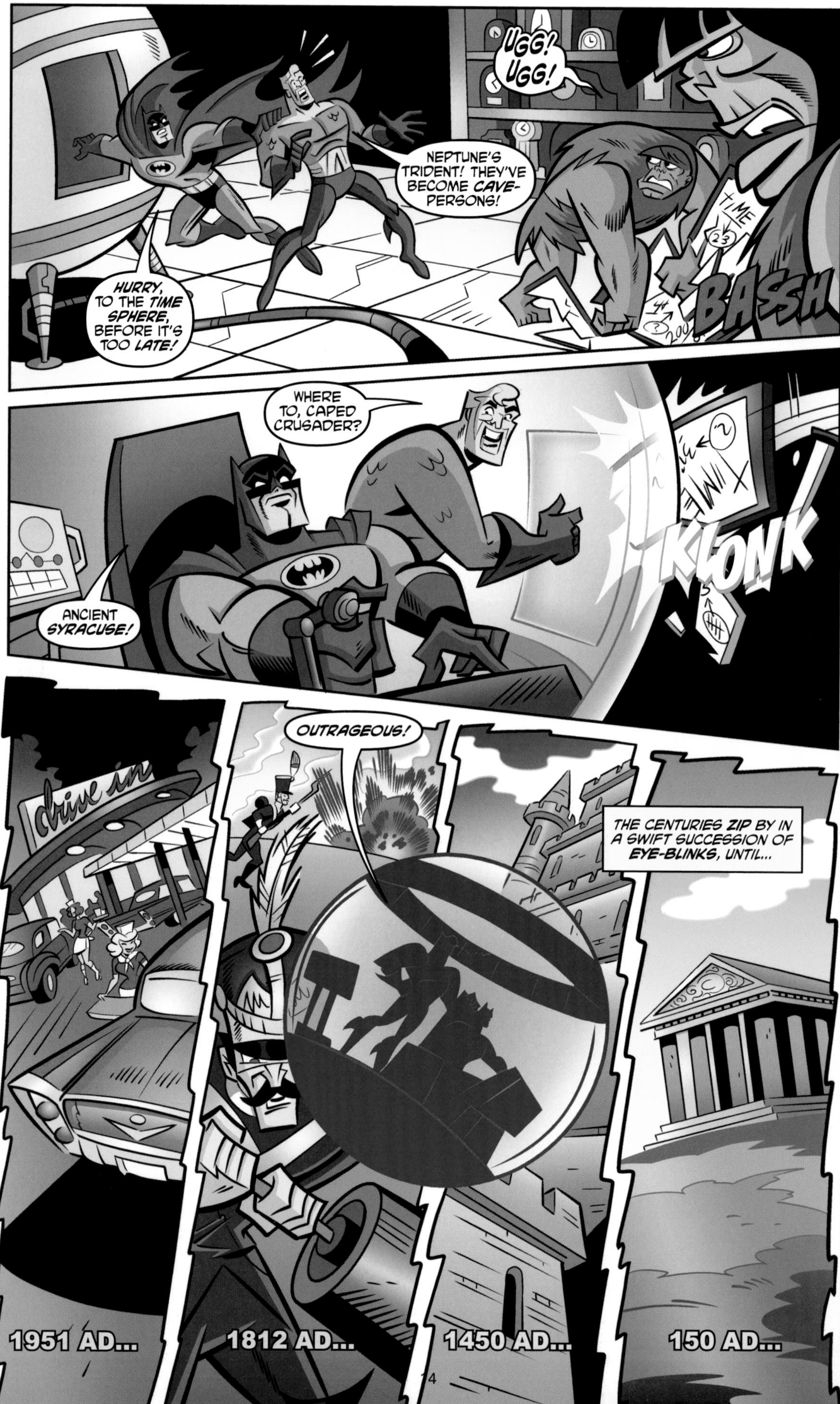
UGG! UGG!
NEPTUNE'S TRIDENT! THEY'VE BECOME CAVE-PERSONS!
HURRY, TO THE TIME SPHERE, BEFORE IT'S TOO LATE!
BASSH
WHERE TO, CAPED CRUSADER?
ANCIENT SYRACUSE!
KLONK
drive in
OUTRAGEOUS!
THE CENTURIES ZIP BY IN A SWIFT SUCCESSION OF EYE-BLINKS, UNTIL...
1951 AD...
1812 AD...
1450 AD...
150 AD...

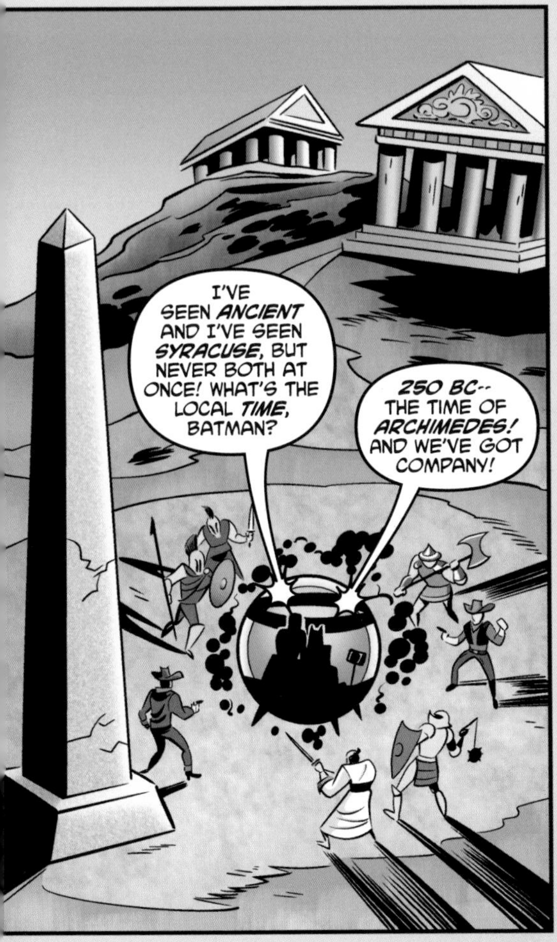
I'VE SEEN ANCIENT AND I'VE SEEN SYRACUSE, BUT NEVER BOTH AT ONCE! WHAT'S THE LOCAL TIME, BATMAN?
250 BC-- THE TIME OF ARCHIMEDES! AND WE'VE GOT COMPANY!

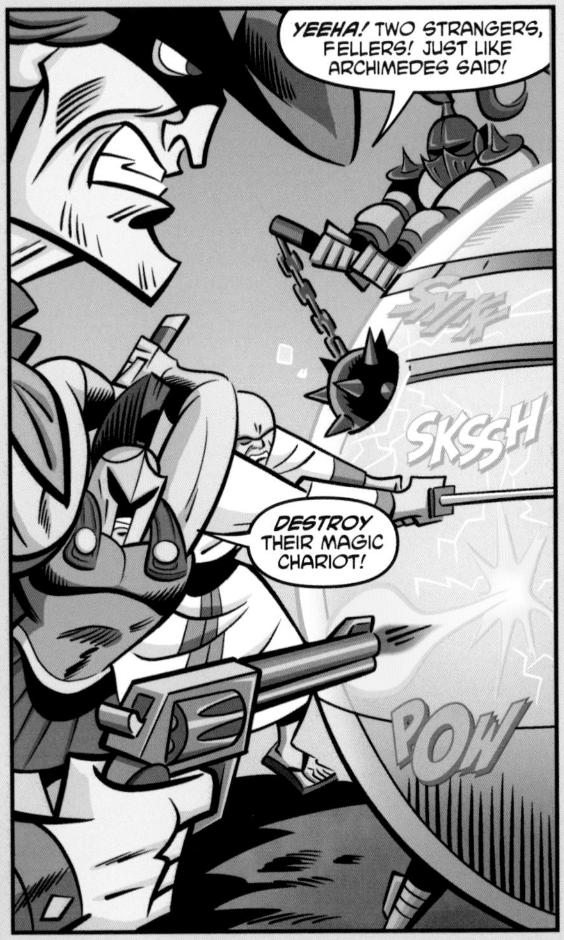
YEEHA! TWO STRANGERS, FELLERS! JUST LIKE ARCHIMEDES SAID!
SNK
SKSSH
DESTROY THEIR MAGIC CHARIOT!
POW

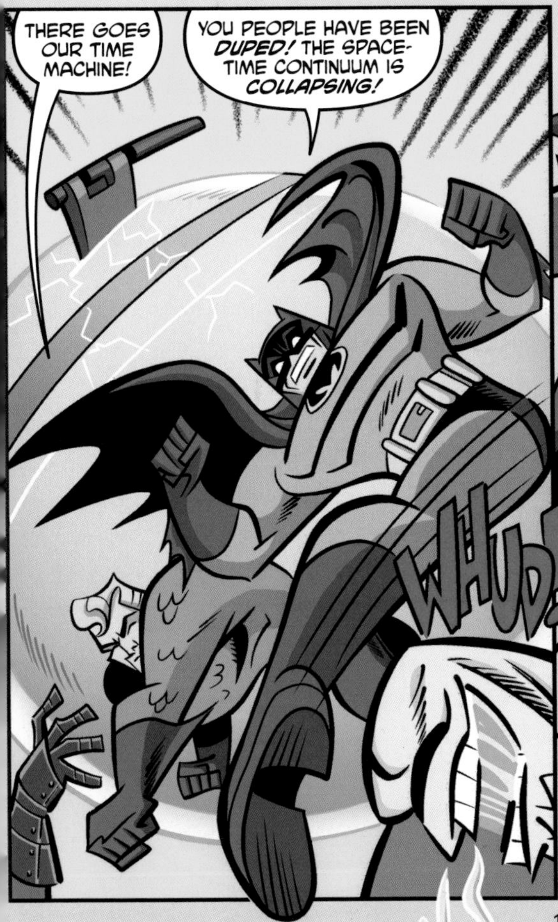
THERE GOES OUR TIME MACHINE!
YOU PEOPLE HAVE BEEN DUPED! THE SPACE-TIME CONTINUUM IS COLLAPSING!
WHUD!

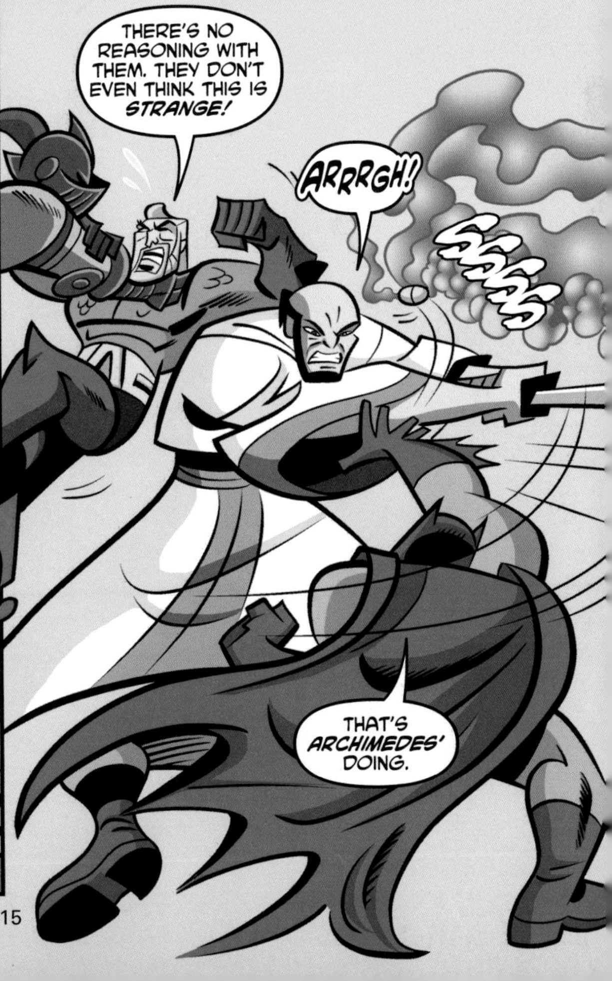
THERE'S NO REASONING WITH THEM. THEY DON'T EVEN THINK THIS IS STRANGE!
ARRRGH!
SSSSS
THAT'S ARCHIMEDES' DOING.

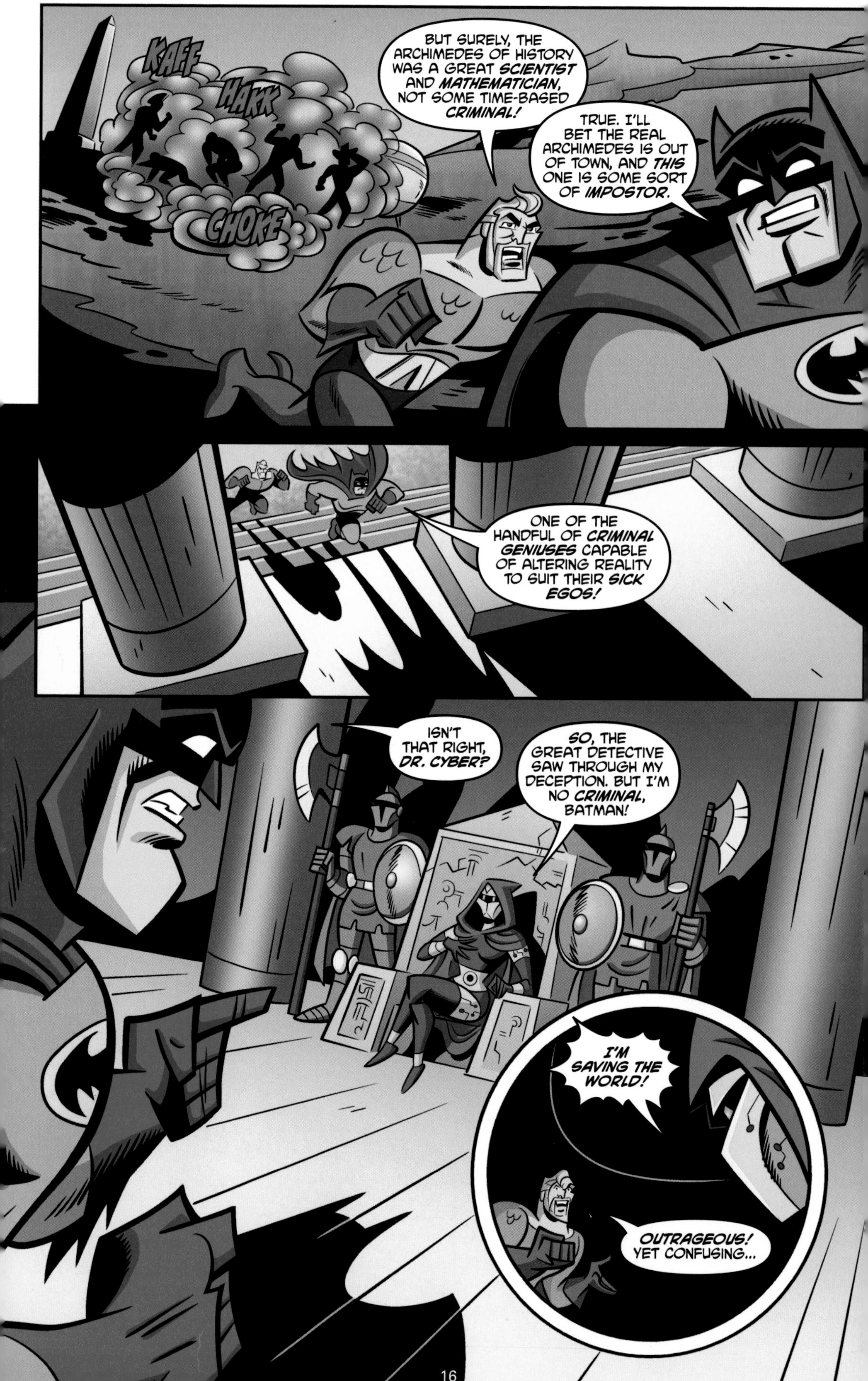
KAFF
HAKK
CHOKE
BUT SURELY, THE ARCHIMEDES OF HISTORY WAS A GREAT SCIENTIST AND MATHEMATICIAN, NOT SOME TIME-BASED CRIMINAL!
TRUE. I'LL BET THE REAL ARCHIMEDES IS OUT OF TOWN, AND THIS ONE IS SOME SORT OF IMPOSTOR.
ONE OF THE HANDFUL OF CRIMINAL GENIUSES CAPABLE OF ALTERING REALITY TO SUIT THEIR SICK EGOS!
ISN'T THAT RIGHT, DR. CYBER?
SO, THE GREAT DETECTIVE SAW THROUGH MY DECEPTION. BUT I'M NO CRIMINAL, BATMAN!
I'M SAVING THE WORLD!
OUTRAGEOUS! YET CONFUSING...

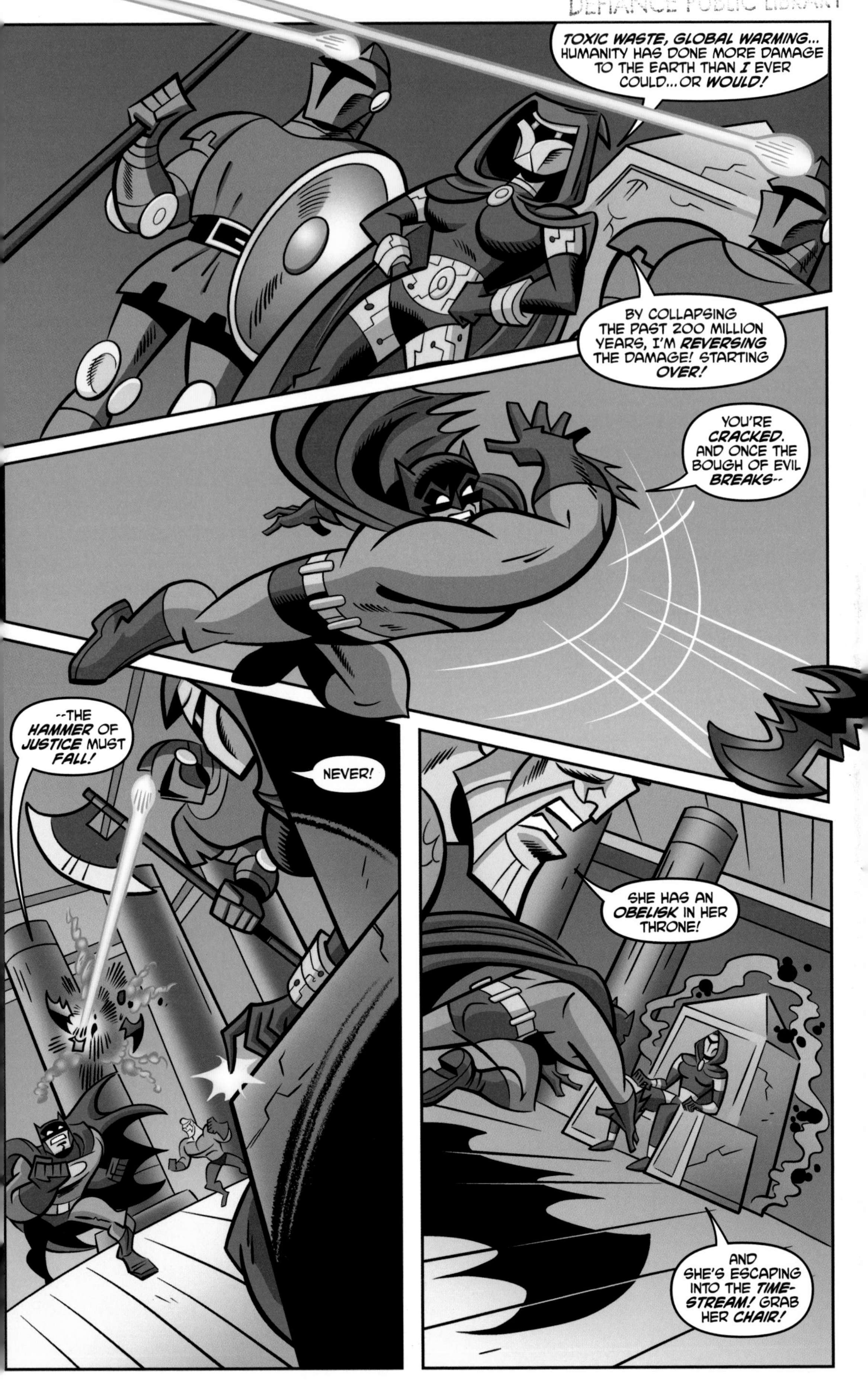
TOXIC WASTE, GLOBAL WARMING... HUMANITY HAS DONE MORE DAMAGE TO THE EARTH THAN I EVER COULD...OR WOULD!
BY COLLAPSING THE PAST 200 MILLION YEARS, I'M REVERSING THE DAMAGE! STARTING OVER!
YOU'RE CRACKED. AND ONCE THE BOUGH OF EVIL BREAKS--
--THE HAMMER OF JUSTICE MUST FALL!
NEVER!
SHE HAS AN OBELISK IN HER THRONE!
AND SHE'S ESCAPING INTO THE TIME-STREAM! GRAB HER CHAIR!

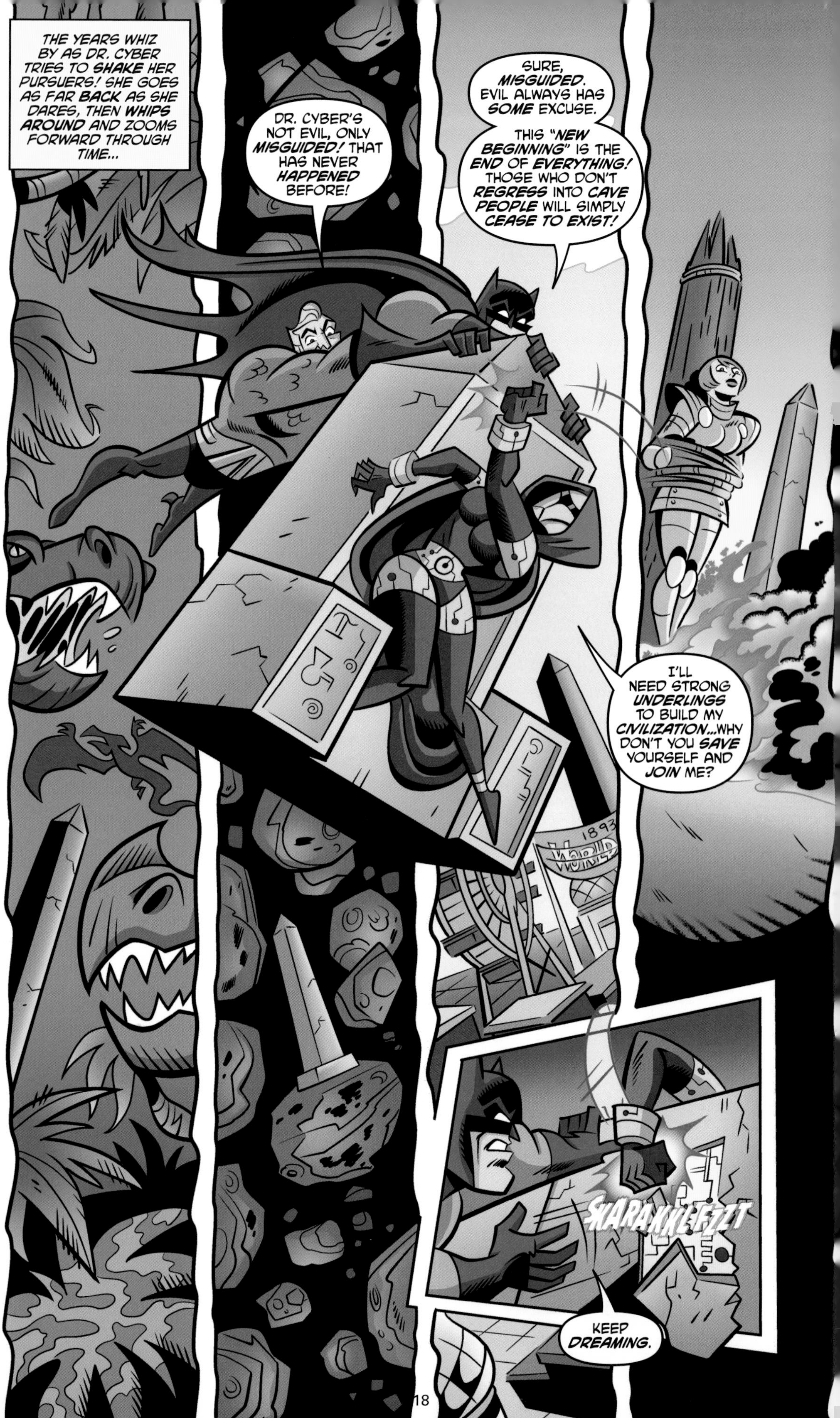
THE YEARS WHIZ BY AS DR. CYBER TRIES TO SHAKE HER PURSUERS! SHE GOES AS FAR BACK AS SHE DARES, THEN WHIPS AROUND AND ZOOMS FORWARD THROUGH TIME...
DR. CYBER'S NOT EVIL, ONLY MISGUIDED! THAT HAS NEVER HAPPENED BEFORE!
SURE, MISGUIDED. EVIL ALWAYS HAS SOME EXCUSE.
THIS "NEW BEGINNING" IS THE END OF EVERYTHING! THOSE WHO DON'T REGRESS INTO CAVE PEOPLE WILL SIMPLY CEASE TO EXIST!
I'LL NEED STRONG UNDERLINGS TO BUILD MY CIVILIZATION...WHY DON'T YOU SAVE YOURSELF AND JOIN ME?
1893
SKARAKKLE-FZZT
KEEP DREAMING.

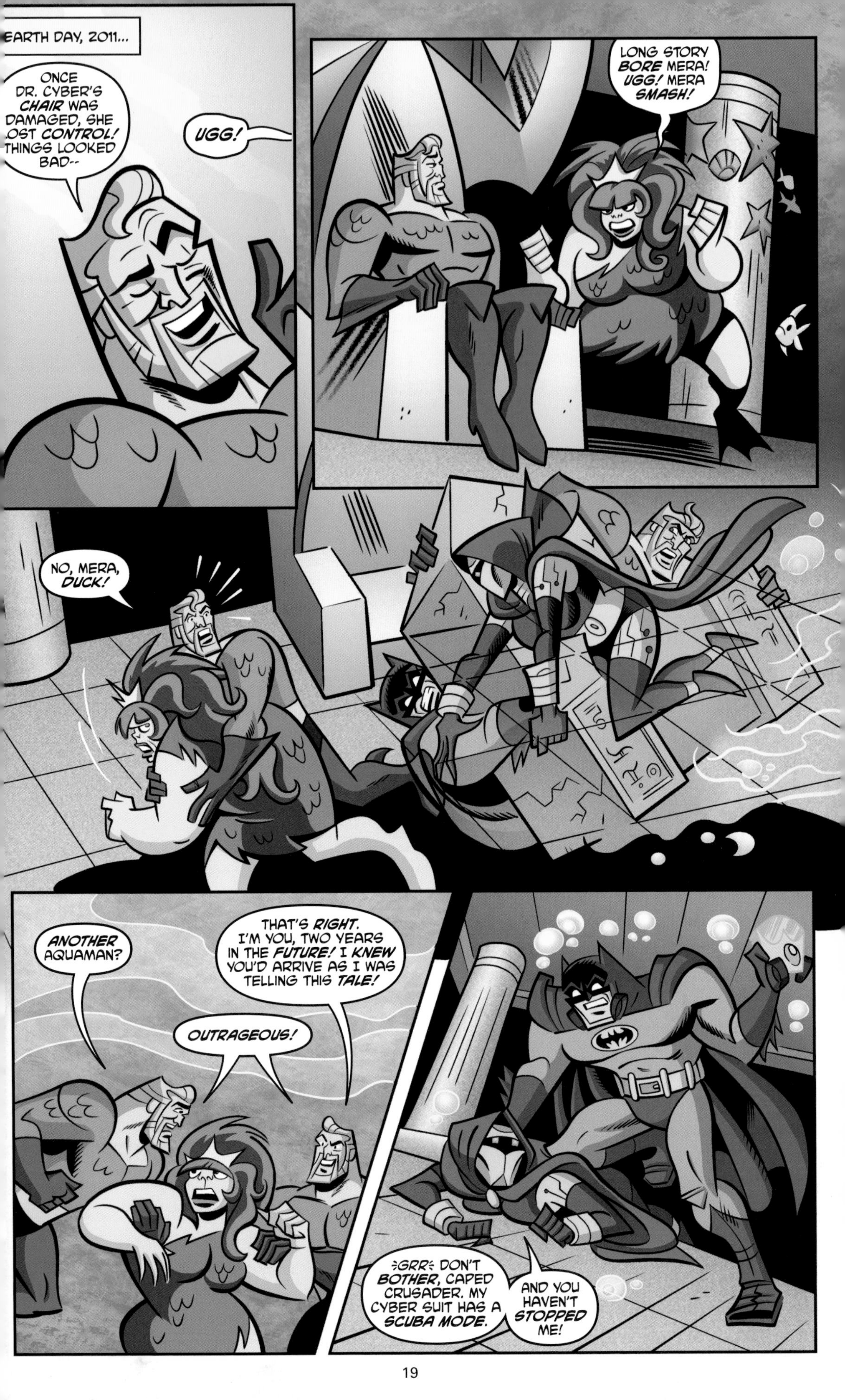
EARTH DAY, 2011...
ONCE DR. CYBER'S CHAIR WAS DAMAGED, SHE LOST CONTROL! THINGS LOOKED BAD--
UGG!
LONG STORY BORE MERA! UGG! MERA SMASH!
NO, MERA, DUCK!
ANOTHER AQUAMAN?
THAT'S RIGHT. I'M YOU, TWO YEARS IN THE FUTURE! I KNEW YOU'D ARRIVE AS I WAS TELLING THIS TALE!
OUTRAGEOUS!
GRR DON'T BOTHER, CAPED CRUSADER. MY CYBER SUIT HAS A SCUBA MODE.
AND YOU HAVEN'T STOPPED ME!

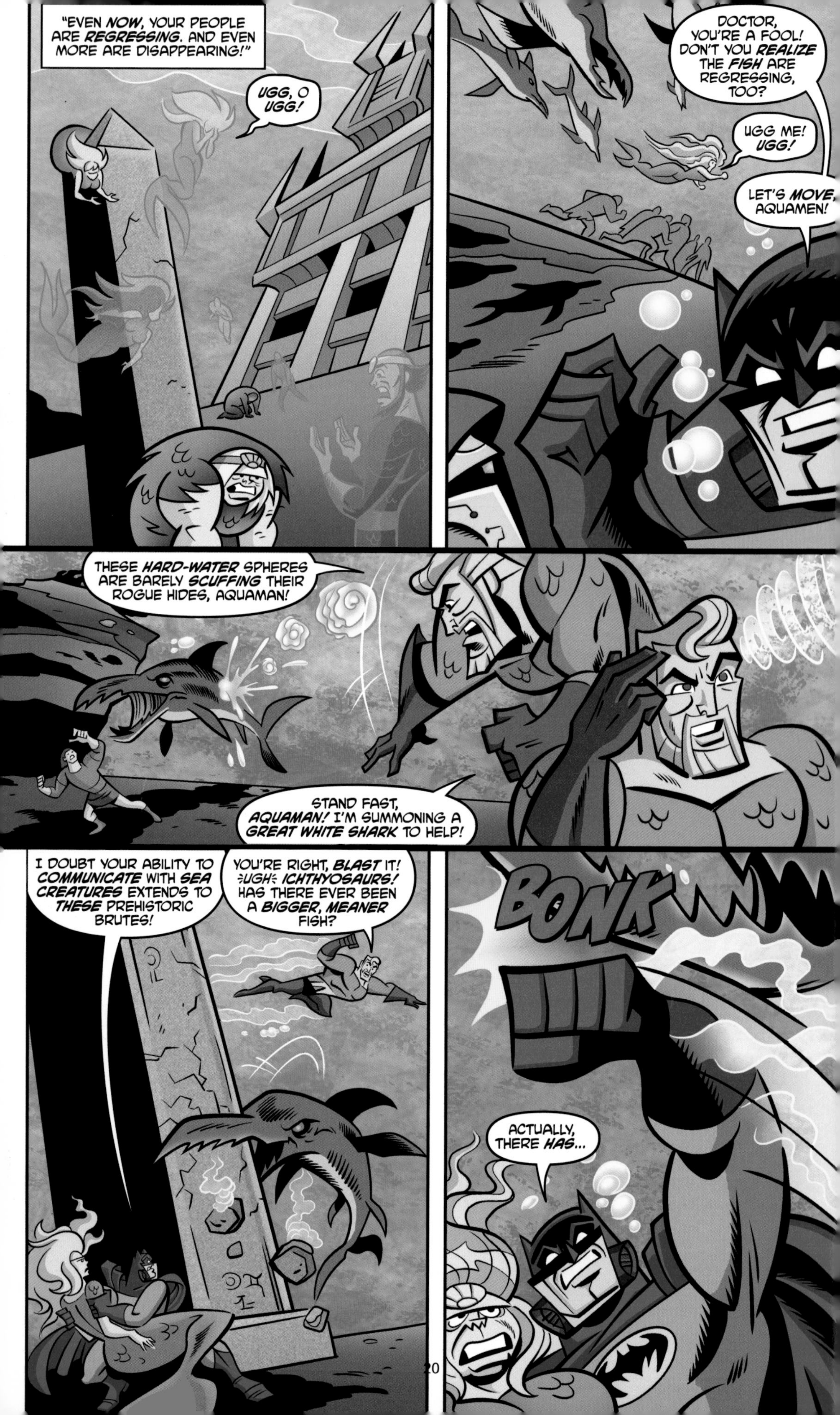

"EVEN NOW, YOUR PEOPLE ARE REGRESSING. AND EVEN MORE ARE DISAPPEARING!"
UGG, O UGG!
DOCTOR, YOU'RE A FOOL! DON'T YOU REALIZE THE FISH ARE REGRESSING, TOO?
UGG ME! UGG!
LET'S MOVE, AQUAMEN!
THESE HARD-WATER SPHERES ARE BARELY SCUFFING THEIR ROGUE HIDES, AQUAMAN!
STAND FAST, AQUAMAN! I'M SUMMONING A GREAT WHITE SHARK TO HELP!
I DOUBT YOUR ABILITY TO COMMUNICATE WITH SEA CREATURES EXTENDS TO THESE PREHISTORIC BRUTES!
YOU'RE RIGHT, BLAST IT! UGH! ICHTHYOSAURS! HAS THERE EVER BEEN A BIGGER, MEANER FISH?
BONK
ACTUALLY, THERE HAS...

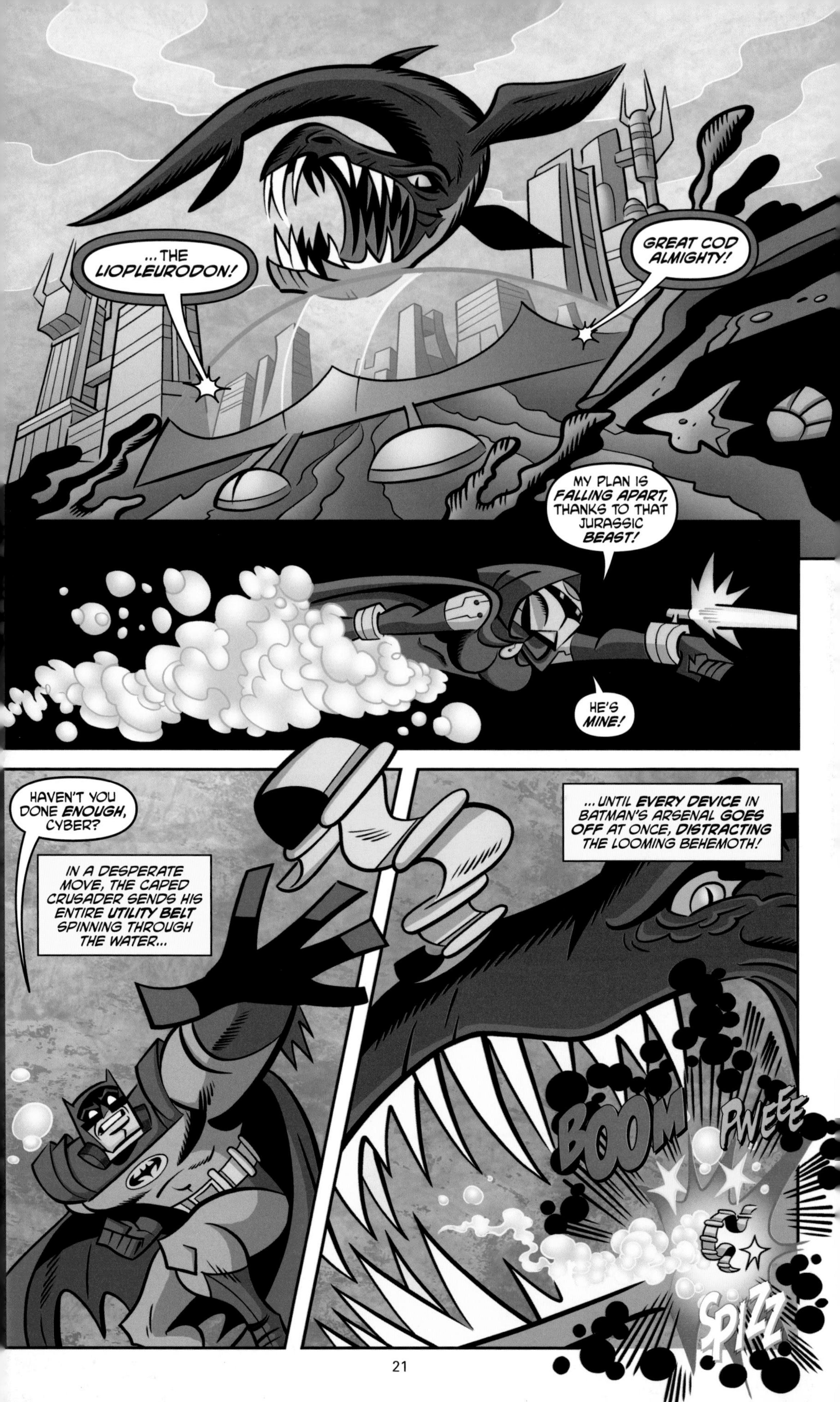
...THE LIOPLEURODON!
GREAT COD ALMIGHTY!
MY PLAN IS FALLING APART, THANKS TO THAT JURASSIC BEAST!
HE'S MINE!
HAVEN'T YOU DONE ENOUGH, CYBER?
IN A DESPERATE MOVE, THE CAPED CRUSADER SENDS HIS ENTIRE UTILITY BELT SPINNING THROUGH THE WATER...
...UNTIL EVERY DEVICE IN BATMAN'S ARSENAL GOES OFF AT ONCE, DISTRACTING THE LOOMING BEHEMOTH!
BOOM
PWEEE
SPIZZ

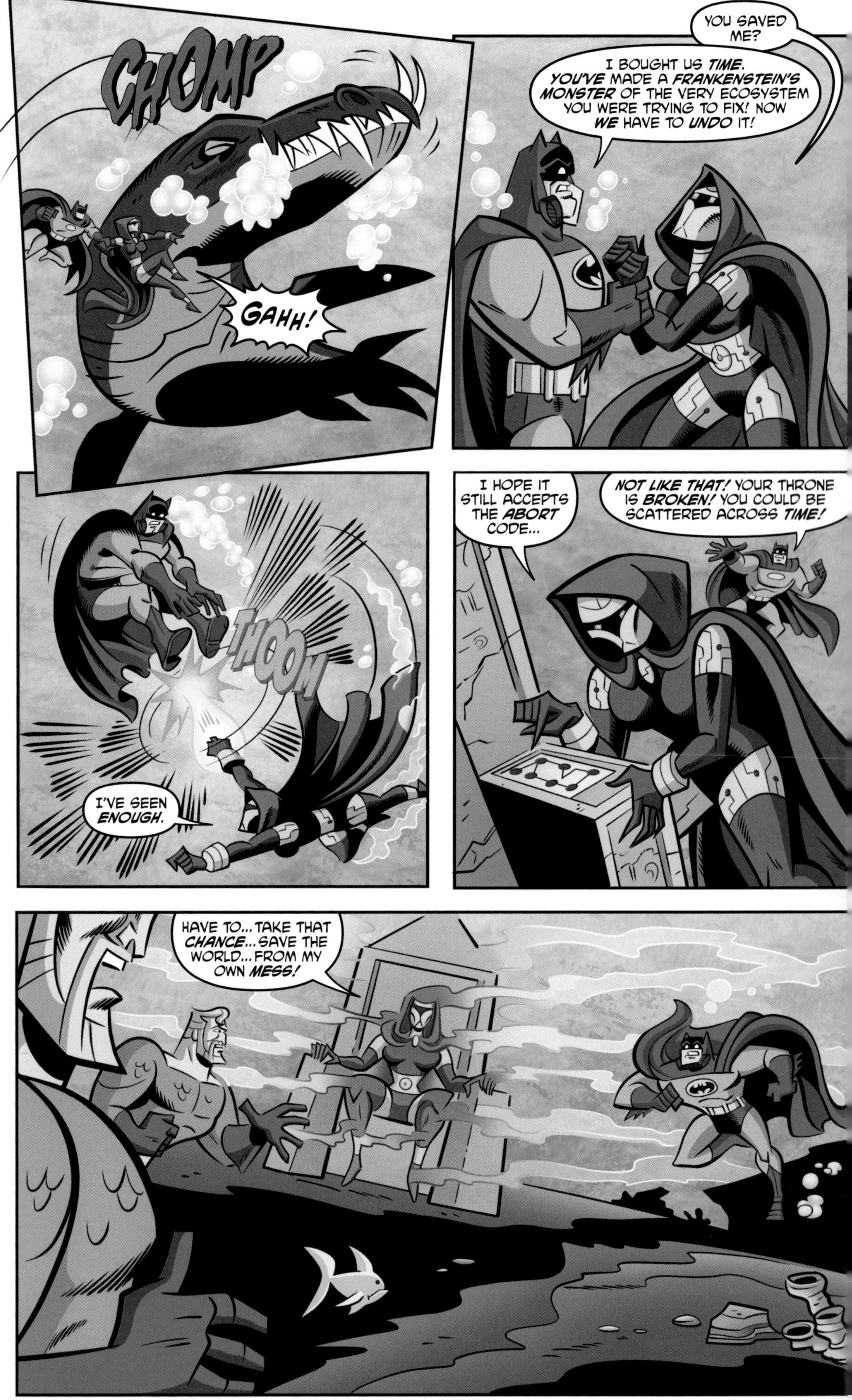
CHOMP
GAHH!
YOU SAVED ME?
I BOUGHT US TIME. YOU'VE MADE A FRANKENSTEIN'S MONSTER OF THE VERY ECOSYSTEM YOU WERE TRYING TO FIX! NOW WE HAVE TO UNDO IT!
THOOM
I'VE SEEN ENOUGH.
I HOPE IT STILL ACCEPTS THE ABORT CODE...
NOT LIKE THAT! YOUR THRONE IS BROKEN! YOU COULD BE SCATTERED ACROSS TIME!
HAVE TO... TAKE THAT CHANCE... SAVE THE WORLD... FROM MY OWN MESS!

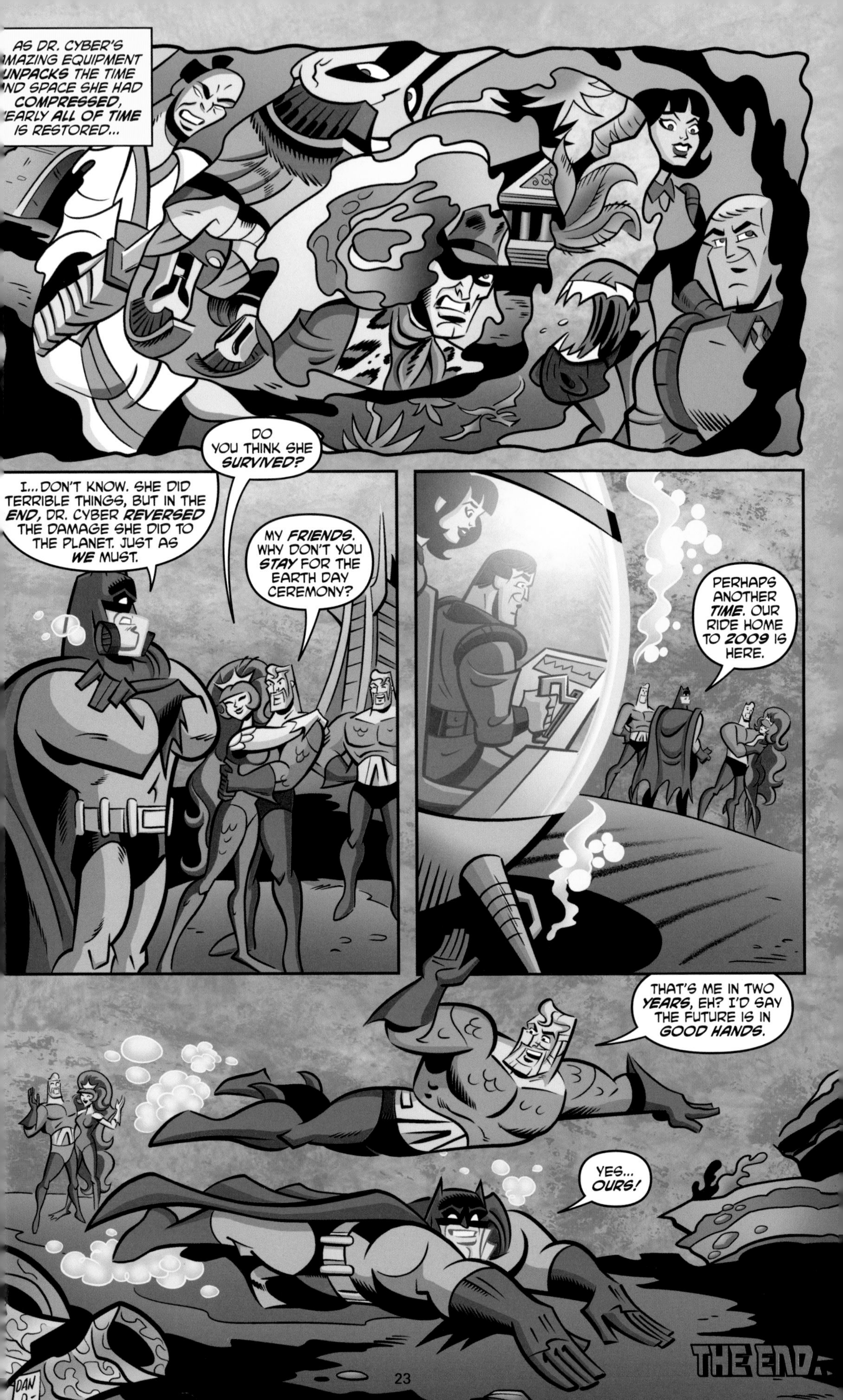
AS DR. CYBER'S AMAZING EQUIPMENT UNPACKS THE TIME AND SPACE SHE HAD COMPRESSED, NEARLY ALL OF TIME IS RESTORED...
DO YOU THINK SHE SURVIVED?
I... DON'T KNOW. SHE DID TERRIBLE THINGS, BUT IN THE END, DR. CYBER REVERSED THE DAMAGE SHE DID TO THE PLANET. JUST AS WE MUST.
MY FRIENDS. WHY DON'T YOU STAY FOR THE EARTH DAY CEREMONY?
PERHAPS ANOTHER TIME. OUR RIDE HOME TO 2009 IS HERE.
THAT'S ME IN TWO YEARS, EH? I'D SAY THE FUTURE IS IN GOOD HANDS.
YES... OURS!
THE END.
DAN D.

DR. CYBER

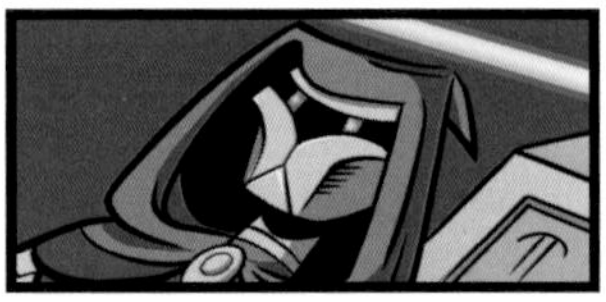

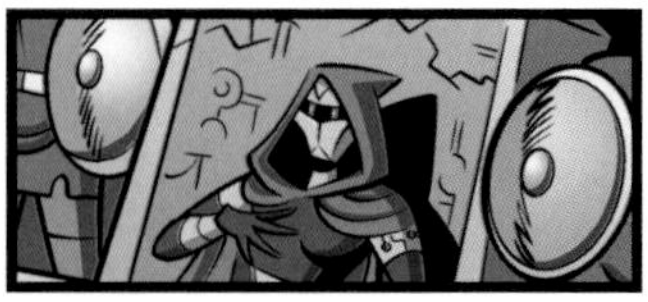

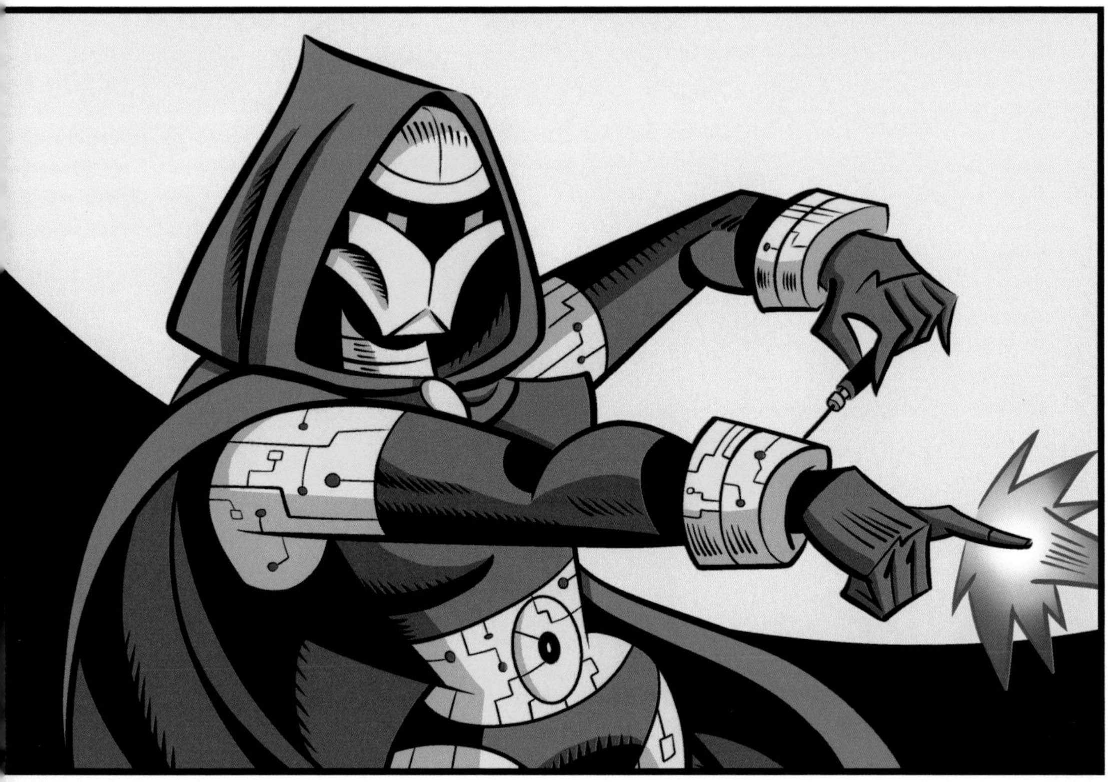

Brilliant Dr. Cyber longs to rule a technological utopia. Using an incredibly advanced cyber suit of her own design, her amazing micro-circuitry can create any number of trans-spatial, dimensional, and temporal effects. Never one to make the same mistake twice, her failed attempts to take over the world always leave her more powerful than before.

TOP SECRET:
For all her technical genius, Dr. Cyber isn't a doctor of science. She holds multiple advanced degrees in literature.

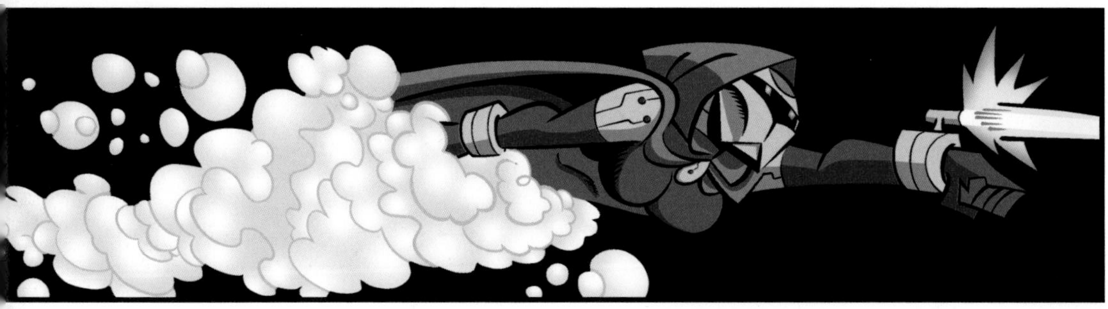

AQUAMAN

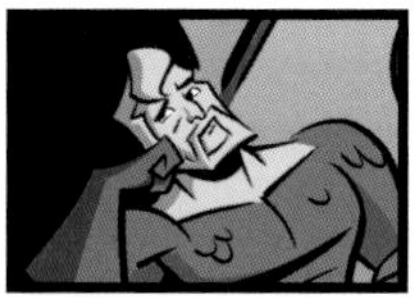

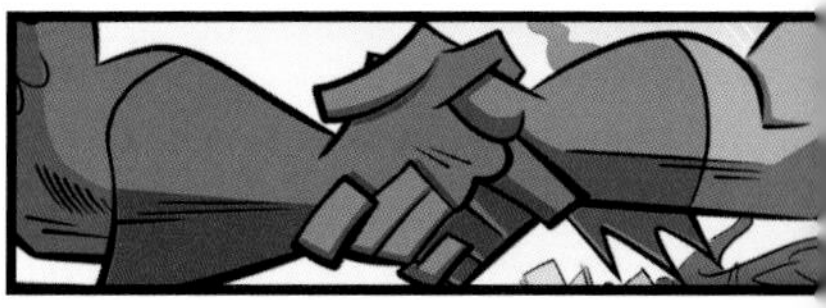

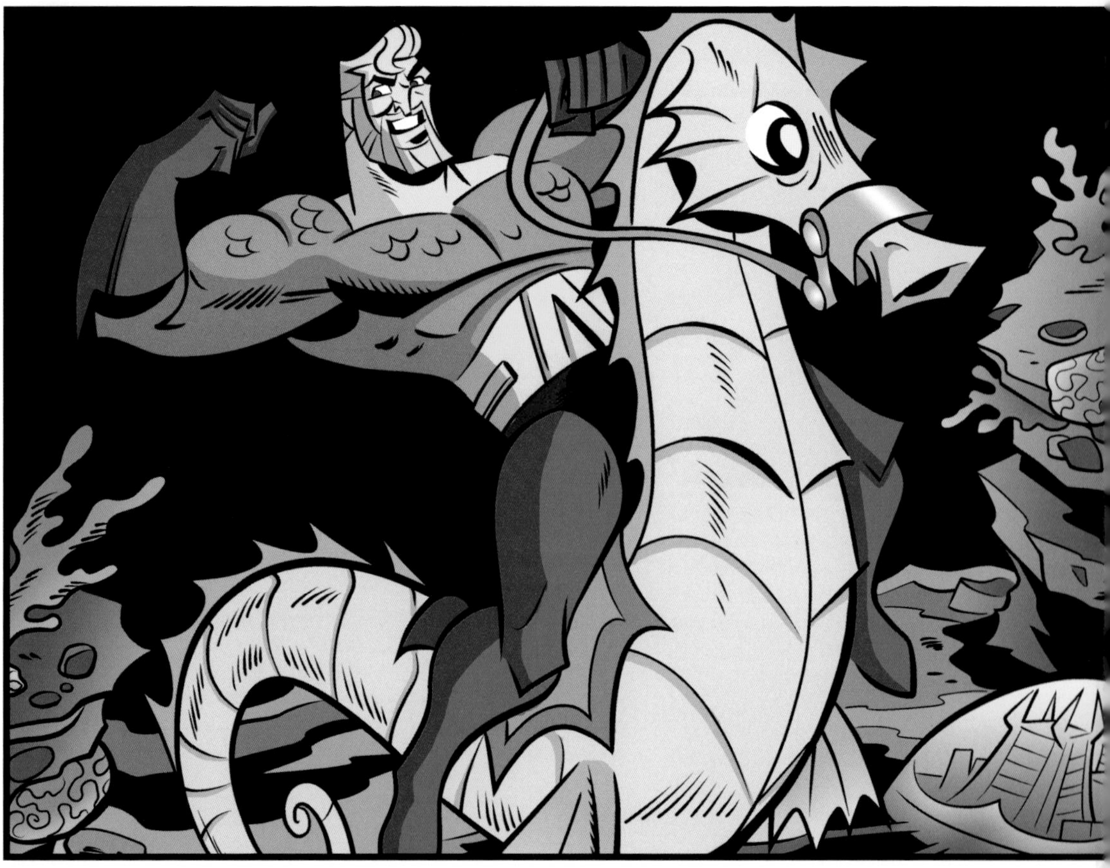

The boisterous undersea King of Atlantis, Aquaman, can swing a whale by the tail, create any number of objects out of "hard-water," and communicate telepathically with sea creatures.

TOP SECRET:
For his amazing abilities, Aquaman can't stop telling you every detail of every one of his adventures.

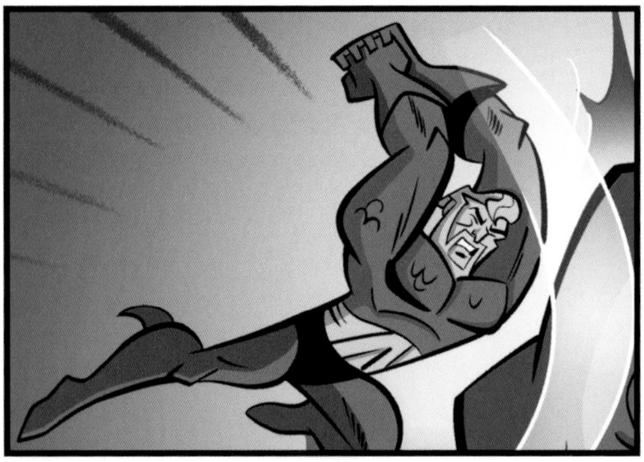

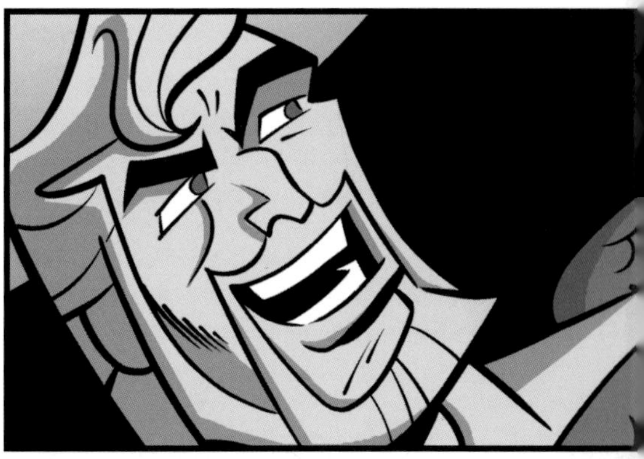

CREATORS

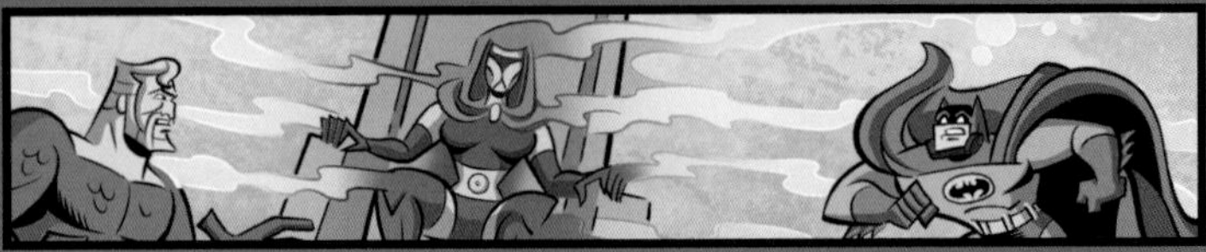

MATT WAYNE WRITER

Matt Wayne is a writer who has worked on TV series including *Ben 10: Ultimate Alien*, *Static Shock*, *Danny Phantom*, and the animated movie *Hellboy: Storm of Swords*. He was an editor at Milestone Media, and has written comics including *Hardware*, *Shadow Cabinet*, *Justice League Unlimited*, and more.

ANDY SURIANO PENCILLER

Andy Suriano is an illustrator of both comic books and animation. His comic book credits include *Batman: The Brave and the Bold* and *Doc Bizarre, M.D.* He's worked on popular animated television series as well, such as *Samurai Jack* and *Star Wars: The Clone Wars.*

DAN DAVIS INKER

Dan Davis is a comic illustrator for DC Comics, Warner Bros., and Bongo. His work has been nominated for several Eisner Awards, including his work on *Batman: The Brave and the Bold*. During his career, Davis has illustrated Batman, The Simpsons, Harry Potter, Samurai Jack, and many other well-known characters!

GLOSSARY

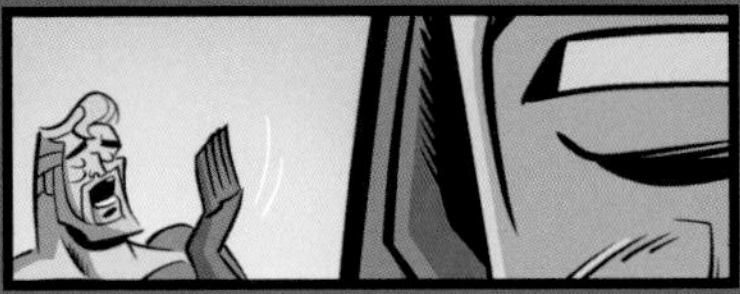

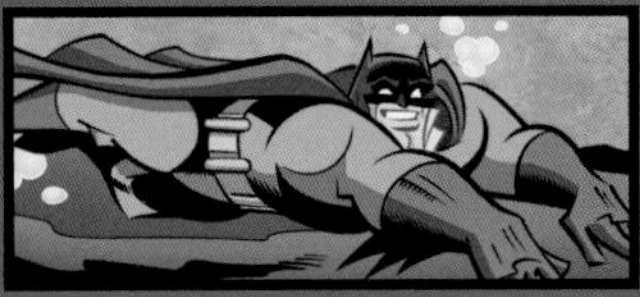

anomalies [uh-NAHM-uh-leez] - things that are different, strange, or not easily described

duped [DOOPT] - deceived or cheated

forbid [fur-BID] - to order someone not to do something

imposter [im-POSS-tur] - someone who pretends to be something he or she is not

obelisk [OB-eh-lisk] - a four-sided pillar that becomes narrower toward the top and ends in a pyramid

regress [ree-GRESS] - to go or cause to go back especially to a previous level

sinister [SIN-uh-stur] - seeming evil and threatening

trident [TRYE-duhnt] - a spear with three prongs

VISUAL QUESTIONS & PROMPTS

1. Super heroes and other comic book characters often have distinctive features. Batman can be recognized even as a baby. Name at least three distinctive physical features of the Dark Knight. Why are these features important?

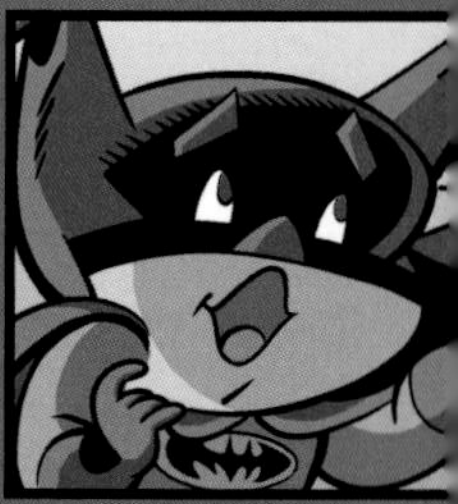

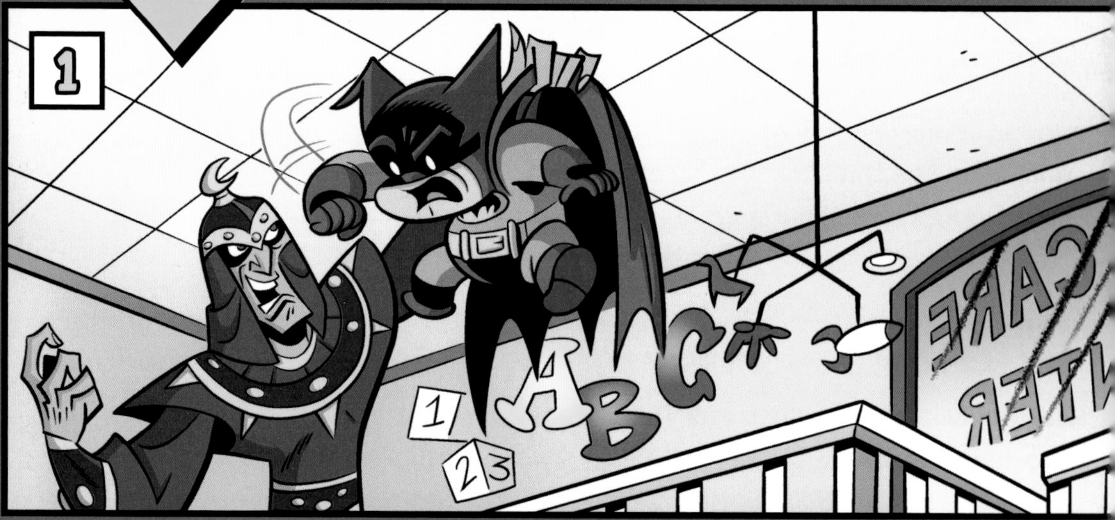
1
A
B
C
1
2
3

2. In comics, the text and illustrations work together to create a complete story. Describe what is happening in the panels below. How did the text and the illustrations help you figure this out?

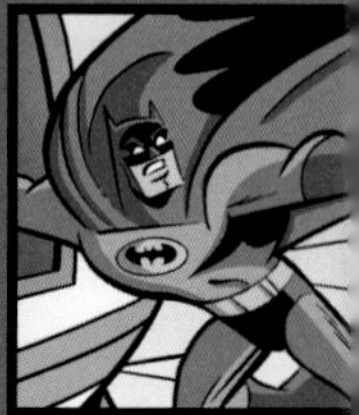

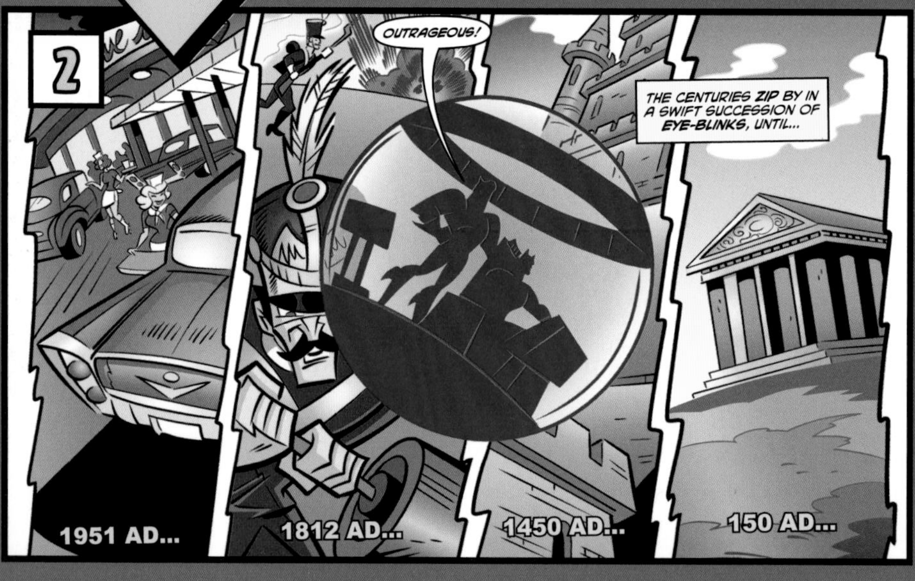
2
1951 AD...
1812 AD...
OUTRAGEOUS!
1450 AD...
THE CENTURIES ZIP BY IN A SWIFT SUCCESSION OF EYE-BLINKS, UNTIL...
150 AD...

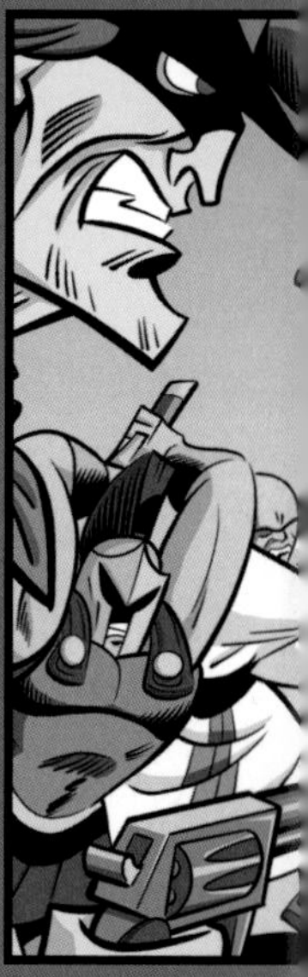

3. The Dark Knight is an expert martial artist. Do you believe he could've solved this problem without using this skill? Why or why not?

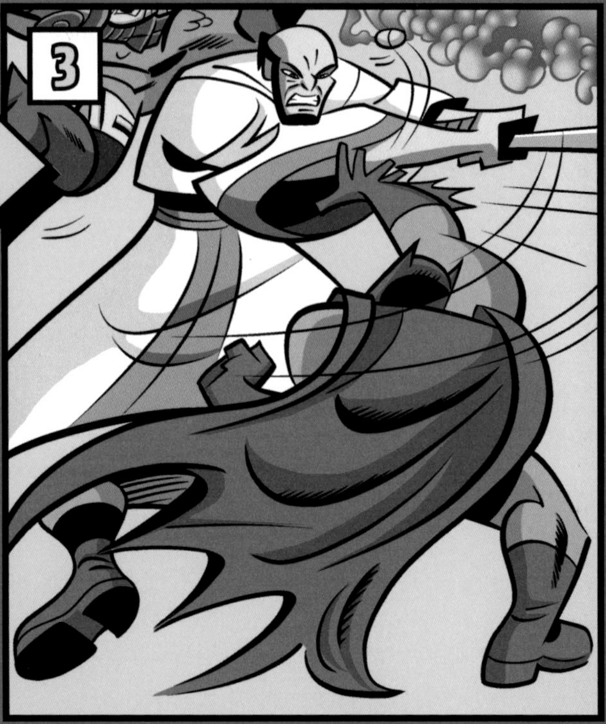
3

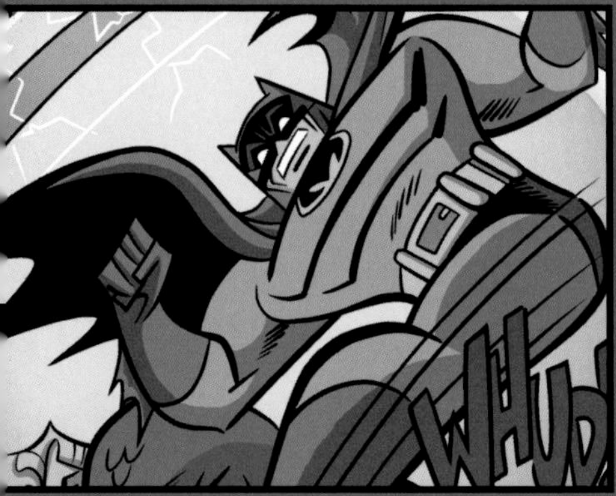
WHUD

4. Batman often uses high-tech devices while solving crimes. Identify two other panels in which Batman uses one of his high-tech gadgets. Describe how these devices could be useful in fighting crime.

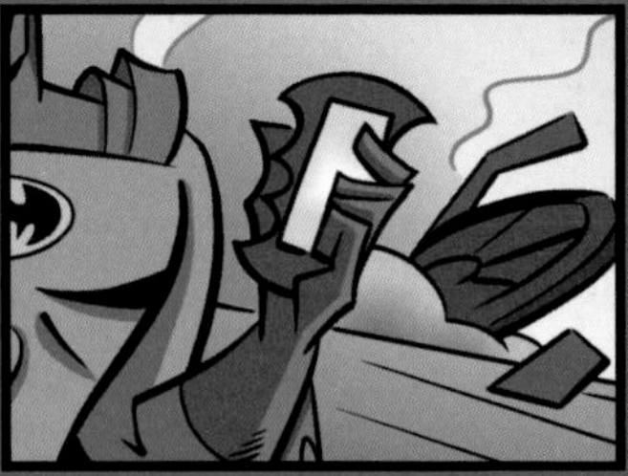

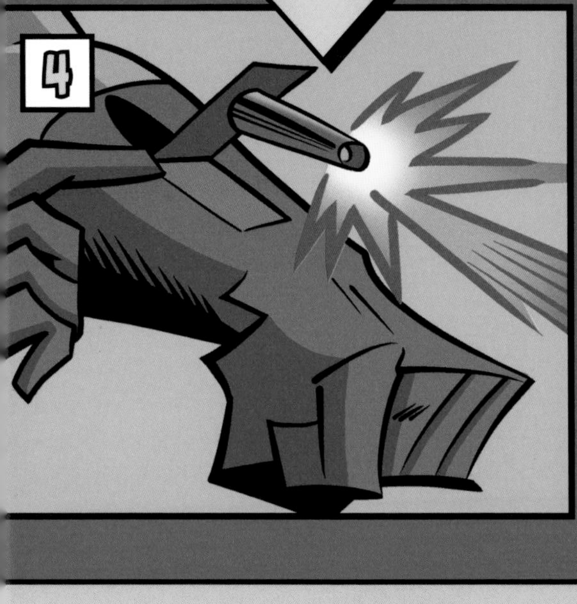
4

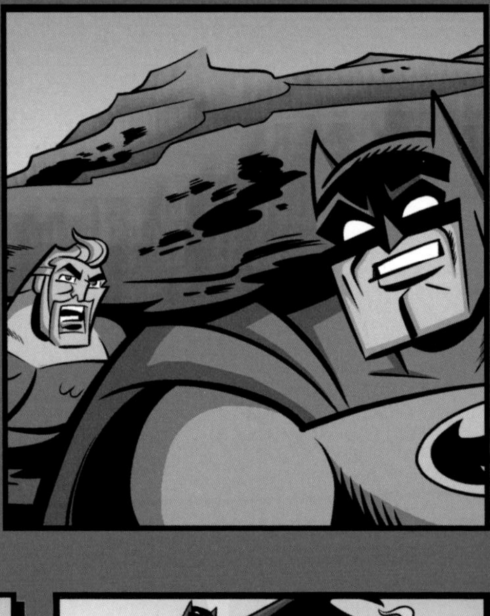

5. Batman teamed up with Aquaman to solve this case. Do you think the Dark Knight could have succeeded alone? Why or why not?

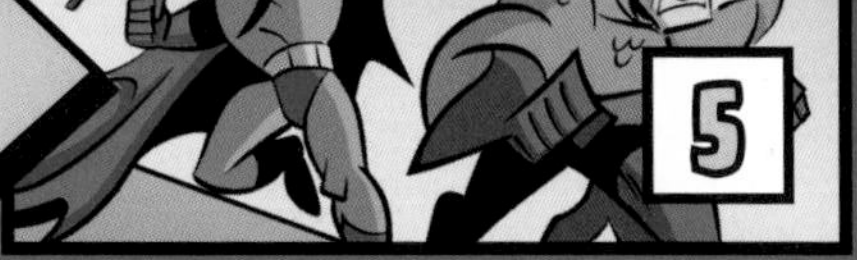
5

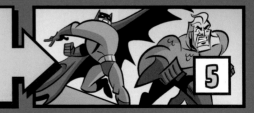

READ THEM ALL!

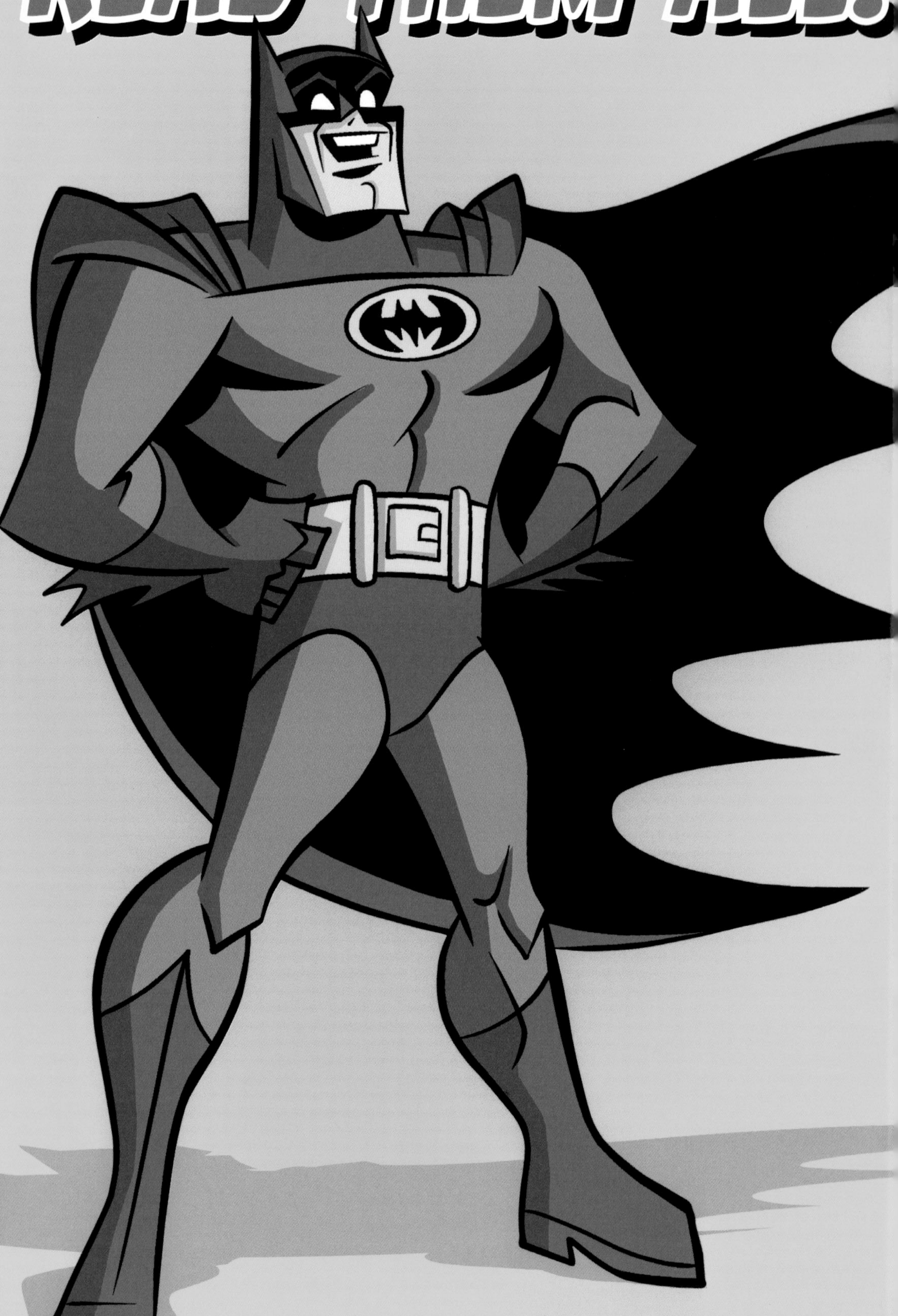

BATMAN
THE BRAVE AND THE BOLD®

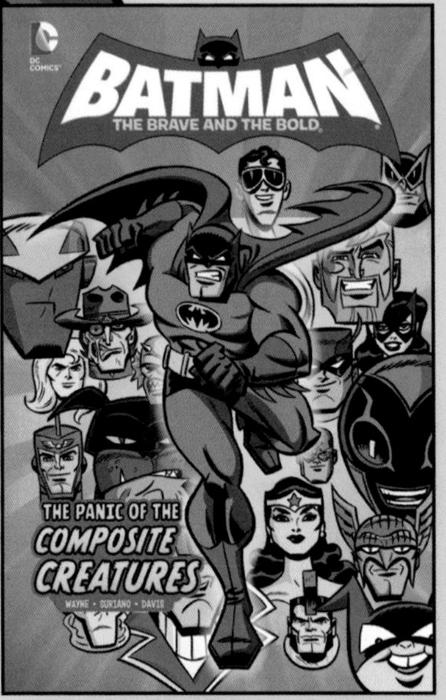
DC COMICS
BATMAN
THE BRAVE AND THE BOLD
THE PANIC OF THE
COMPOSITE CREATURES
WAYNE • SURIANO • DAVIS
THE PANIC OF THE COMPOSITE CREATURES

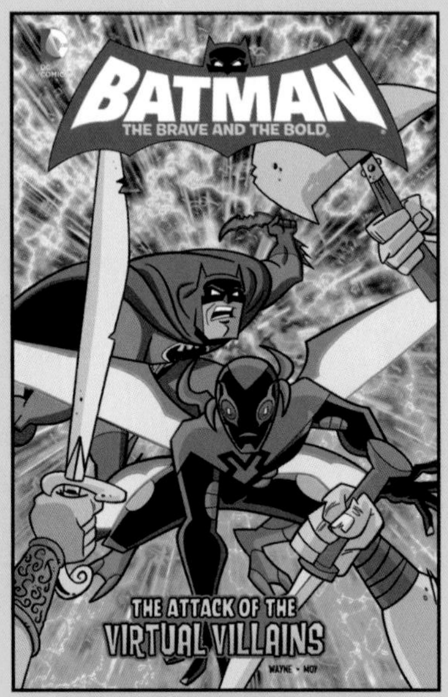
BATMAN
THE BRAVE AND THE BOLD
THE ATTACK OF THE
VIRTUAL VILLAINS
THE ATTACK OF THE VIRTUAL VILLAINS

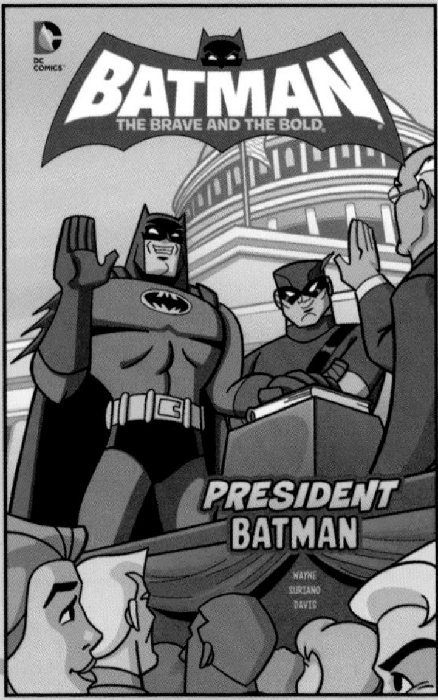
DC COMICS
BATMAN
THE BRAVE AND THE BOLD
PRESIDENT
BATMAN
WAYNE
SURIANO
DAVIS
PRESIDENT BATMAN

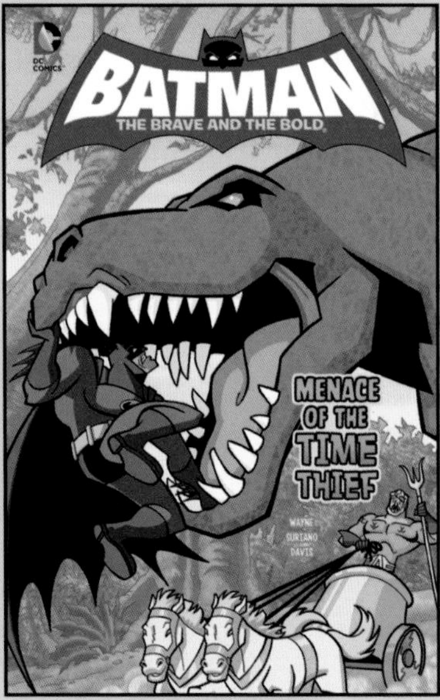
DC COMICS
BATMAN
THE BRAVE AND THE BOLD
MENACE
OF THE
TIME
THIEF
WAYNE
SURIANO
DAVIS
MENACE OF THE TIME THIEF

ONLY FROM...

STONE ARCH BOOKS™
a capstone imprint www.capstonepub.com